I0746100

ROCKY ROAD DREAMS

The Candy Beach Series – Book 5

Cecelia Dowdy

Melanie used to be love with Kyle's identical twin. Could she really have feelings for Kyle - or does she like him because he reminds her of his brother?

Kyle Baxter had a secret crush on Melanie Richards for years, but she was smitten with his identical twin brother, Keith. Recently sober, he takes a Christmas-time hiatus from his law firm. He rents a beach house - right across the street from Melanie. As he uncovers secrets about his past, he's determined to learn more about his mother who died when he was a baby.

Obese as a child, Melanie Richards is now slender and beautiful. She owns an herbal health food store. Having her own business comes with a high price. Her uncle agrees to finance her shop as long as she agrees to mentor Chloe, her drunken, wayward, 21-year-old cousin. Chloe's erratic behavior wreaks havoc in Melanie's life. Can a Christmas road trip help them to solve Kyle's and Chloe's problems? Is Melanie attracted to Kyle because he resembles his twin, or does she love Kyle for himself?

Dowdy writes with the right touch to keep the readers engaged and vested... - USA Today

Sign up for Cecelia Dowdy's email list :

https://ceceliadowdy.com/sign-up-for-my-email-list/

Rocky Road DREAMS

For more information, or to book an event, contact : cecelia@ceceliadowdy.com & ceceliadowdy.com

Published by Divine Desserts Publishing LLC
Cover design by Elizabeth Mackey Graphics
Coffee Cup Image : Watercolor Christmas Illustration with Blue Cup by Natali Brill
ISBN - Paperback: 978-1-7338926-8-1
First Edition: January 2022

1

M an, this was hard.

Kyle Baxter paced on Melanie Richard's front porch, clutching the store-bought cheesecake he'd purchased for Thanksgiving dessert. He stopped pacing and gulped, set the cheesecake on the ledge, and wiped his damp palms on his pants.

Ridiculous. He'd known Melanie for most of his life, so, why should he feel so nervous about seeing her today? *Lord, give me the courage to talk to Melanie. I want her to see me as a new man.* Might as well get this over with. He grabbed the cheesecake just as the first notes of Nat King Cole's *A Christmas Song* crooned through the closed door. A memory, fresh and vivid as newly fallen snow, wrapped through his mind. He recalled his dad telling him once that this was his mom's favorite song.

Pushing the memory away, he knocked on the door, silently singing along with the song. Hopefully the music would help to calm his frazzled nerves.

"Coming." Oh, how he loved the sound of Melanie's voice. She opened the door. Whoa. Speechless. She was prettier than the last time he'd seen her – which, he reckoned was about five years ago when he'd been pumped up on alcohol every night. Her nut-brown skin glowed in the early afternoon sunlight. She grinned, showing off her perfect white teeth. He remembered her when she'd been an overweight kid, sporting braces, stating that she wished she looked like the models she'd seen in magazines.

Well, in his opinion, her wish had come true. "Kyle, it's so good to see you." Well good thing she wasn't annoyed that he was over an hour early. Before he could say anything, she hugged him. He gave her a hard, one-armed hug since he was still holding the cheesecake in one hand. She smelled delicious. Like flowers and lemon. Liquid warmth filled him. The urge to kiss her slammed through him like a freight train. Startled, he pulled away.

He swallowed, still clutching the Saran-wrapped cheesecake. He managed to smile. "Hey, Melanie. I finally made it into town for my vacation this afternoon." Vacation was an understatement. He supposed he could call his break from work a vacation. Sort of.

She glanced at her watch. "You're early."

He shrugged. "Sorry." His heart continued to pound wildly. Hopefully he'd calm down soon. He presented her with his after-dinner gift. "I thought we could eat this after supper."

She glanced down at the cheesecake, and her smile faltered. She groaned. "Oh, I love cheesecake." She shook her head and beckoned him inside. "But I don't know if I can indulge." She patted her flat stomach. "I'm trying to keep trim and cheesecake is not on my list of foods."

Before he could comment she touched his arm. As Nat King Cole continued singing in the background, she leaned toward him. "It's great to see you again, Kyle. It's been too long." Her beautiful dark brown eyes sparkled. Joy flowed through him like liquid honey. She really was glad to see him. He could see it. His nervousness evaporated. Maybe they'd have a nice dinner after all.

Maybe over the next month, over the Christmas season, he could finally find the courage to tell her his true feelings. "It's good to see you, too." He glanced at her before setting the cheesecake on the table. He recalled when they were kids, when she'd been pudgy, how she'd gobbled cheesecake as if there were no tomorrow. She'd revealed to him once that she'd die if cheesecake were to disappear from this God-given earth.

He took a deep breath and eyed the counter. Fake evergreen and tiny lights decorated the rim of the kitchen workspace. Amidst the greenery, he spotted an open bottle of wine. He squeezed his eyes shut. Oh no. He should've been honest with her, had a talk, told her about his recent sobriety. He inwardly sighed. Hopefully, she wasn't planning on serving alcohol during their meal. He finally opened his eyes and looked away from the beverage, ashamed of his weakness.

He focused on Melanie at the stove, stirring a pot of food. The enticing scent of tomatoes, herbs and spices filled the air. His mouth watered. He'd focus on the food. Get his mind off of the alcohol sitting on the counter. "What're you cooking? Smells good."

"We're having turkey meat loaf with my special tomato sauce." She gestured toward the oven. "The meat loaf is in the oven. I'm cooking the tomato sauce on the stove. Cooking a turkey seemed wasteful since there's only three of us for dinner." She placed her spoon back on the stove and placed the lid over the simmering pot. "So, what have you been up to lately?"

He shrugged. "Not much. I've got a lot on my mind." He still missed his Alcoholics Anonymous sponsor Earl. Earl had been like a brother to him. Earl's passing was part of the reason why he'd ended up taking a one-month work hiatus on the Outer Banks. He didn't want to talk about his AA sponsor during dinner. Maybe he'd mention him to Melanie later – after they'd gotten to know one another better. He plopped into a chair. Hopefully this dinner would end on a positive note. The Nat King Cole song ended, and *Jingle Bell Rock* now played through the speakers.

"You can tell me all about what's on your mind during dinner."

A young pretty, brown-skinned woman sauntered into the kitchen and lifted the wine bottle. Her voice slurred while she tried to sing along to *Jingle Bell Rock*.

She sounded awful.

The young woman poured the rose-colored liquid into her empty glass and took a huge gulp. "Hey, you must be Kyle." Oh, no. This woman was sloshed. Maybe he shouldn't have accepted Melanie's Thanksgiving dinner invitation. She held her hand toward him. "I'm Chloe. Melanie's cousin."

Kyle shook her hand. "Nice to meet you."

"Chloe, why don't you go back upstairs?" Melanie's voice hardened as Chloe narrowed her eyes.

"Why?" She sauntered around the table and hummed along to the music. She eyed Kyle. "Hey, you kinda cute. You need to get rid of that beard, though. I don't like beards on men."

"Chloe…" Sounded like Melanie was giving Chloe a warning.

"Oh, shut up already, Mel. Your loud voice is makin' my head hurt." She made herself comfortable in a chair beside Kyle. She took a gulp of wine.

He wanted to suggest she stop drinking but doubted she'd listen. Chloe continued drinking, tapping her foot, singing to Christmas carols off-key. The scent of her overpowering perfume poisoned the air. Whew, the smell almost made him lose his appetite. Maybe when she sobered up Melanie could tell Chloe not to wear so much fragrance.

Perhaps he could go outside a bit and say that he needed some air. He was about to get up when Melanie brought the food to the table. She leaned toward Kyle. "Sorry about Chloe." She whispered the words into his ear so that Chloe would not hear her.

Chloe's eyes were closed as she tapped her

foot and listened to the Christmas music. Her eyes shot open. She looked right at him. Chloe grinned and stood on her high-heeled shoes and leaned towards him while her tight shirt strained against her chest. "Would you like a drink?" Her voice slurred as she lost her balance. The red liquid shot out of the glass and splashed onto Kyle's face.

"Ugh!" A river of wine spilled into his mouth and the sweet alluring taste beckoned him, warming his tongue and throat, making him want to guzzle several glasses of the forbidden drink. Unable to help himself, he licked a few stray drops from his lips. Man, this wine tasted so good. *He had to keep his sobriety.* Just calm down and do not focus on the alcohol. Earl's advice popped into his head. He jumped up and bumped the table. A glass toppled onto the floor and shattered into pieces.

"Chloe." Melanie's voice cracked throughout the kitchen like a clap of thunder. "Kyle, I'm so sorry."

Heaven help him. He needed to do something before he lost his mind. Melanie pressed a wad of napkins into his hand. He mopped the wine from his face. He had to get some air. He left the table as shards of glass crunched beneath his shoes. He went through Melanie's small, fragrant herb shop toward her back deck. He pushed the doors open. The warmth from the sun and waves crashing on the beach made him feel a bit better. Felt good to smell the fresh briny air. The wind picked up and blew across the water on the outer banks of North Carolina.

He closed his eyes and lifted his head toward the sky. The unseasonably warm sun felt so good. Chloe's childish laughter echoed from the kitchen. He wondered if she got drunk often. How did Melanie put up with this?

Melanie followed him outside. She touched his shoulder. "Sorry, Kyle. I hope Chloe didn't ruin your Thanksgiving."

He wasn't sure what to say. He took a deep breath and dropped into a two-person deck chair. He needed to calm down. He figured Melanie thought he was strange since he'd rushed out of the kitchen. To relieve his anxiety he closed his eyes and took several deep breaths – just as they'd taught him in rehab. After he'd calmed down he opened his eyes.

"Are you sick?" She looked worried. He figured she wasn't used to seeing him do his deep breathing exercises.

He shook his head. He supposed he could be called *sick* but not in the way Melanie was probably thinking. His alcoholism was like an incurable disease. "Is your cousin old enough to drink?" She looked like a teenager. He figured Melanie wouldn't have an underaged drinker in her house, but he had to ask. Thoughts of how he'd started drinking as a teen filled his mind. No way did he want Chloe to start relying on alcohol at such a young age. He wanted to help if he could.

"Chloe is twenty-one but she still acts like a child. I'm sorry she spilled wine on you. She's never acted this bad when she's drunk before."

He took a few minutes to digest what she'd said. He focused on the golden, bright orange sun as it set on the waves crashing upon the sandy white beach. Melanie dropped into the seat beside him. He took another deep breath and resisted the urge to hold her hand. He needed to tell her the truth. There was no reason for him to hide his weakness. "I didn't leave the table because of Chloe. It's the wine I can't stand. It's hard for me to be around alcohol."

"I remember you used to drink a lot."

His life had been a mess. Surprising that Melanie welcomed him into her home like this. He'd caused his twin brother Keith a lot of worry when he'd been drunk. He could only imagine what Keith had told Melanie about his drinking problem over the years.

"I've been sober for a few months now." He swallowed and folded his hands in front of his chest. "I had a bad drinking problem and recently I've found the courage to finally stop." Well, he'd gotten sober a few *years* ago. But that all changed when Earl died. He'd fallen off the wagon and he was ashamed of that.

Melanie squeezed his shoulder. "That's wonderful, I didn't realize---"

He turned toward her, cutting her off, trying not to stare into her dark eyes. Her smooth skin looked appealing in the late afternoon sunlight. He longed to touch the small mole above her upper lip. "There are lots of things about me you don't know. It's been years since we we've spent any time together." His identical twin brother Keith used to be Melanie's best friend for years. Oh, how he'd envied Keith's connection with Melanie.

"Kyle, you coming back in here?" Chloe's slurred voice carried onto the back deck. Melanie winced.

"I'm sorry about Chloe," she repeated. "She was a little upset earlier when she was talking on the phone to one of her friends. She disappeared in her room for a couple of hours before dinner. I had no idea she was drinking the whole time she was upstairs."

He touched her shoulder. "Don't be sorry." He swallowed. The intoxicating taste of the wine lingered on his tongue. He needed to get rid of it, fast. He'd noticed a liquor store when he'd first arrived in town. The urge to visit the store to purchase some booze swept through him. He figured Melanie knew how ugly he used to act when he was intoxicated. He glanced at her profile, realizing he needed to gain her trust before he revealed everything about himself.

She patted his shoulder. "You'll need to tell me more about what's been happening with you. I'm surprised Keith didn't tell me this."

Kyle balled his hands into fists. "Do you still talk to Keith regularly?" He hoped that Melanie's affection for his identical twin brother would've dwindled since he was now married with children.

She shook her head. "I don't really talk to him much anymore but we email each other sometimes. He sent me pictures of his twin babies when they were born."

"Oh, good." Relief swept through him. He cleared his throat as the breeze blew, sending waves of coolness over his heated skin. Nervous, he placed his hands into his pockets, tilting his head toward the double doors. "I can't stomach eating dinner with your cousin if she'll be drinking like that. I'll eat at home."

Melanie stood and walked toward the doors. "I don't blame you. I'm wondering what I've gotten myself into, living here with Chloe." She looked directly into his eyes, changing the subject. "Do you like the house across the street that you rented from my cousin Dale for your vacation?"

He nodded. "It's nice, functional. It's a great place to stay for a month."

"Good." She paused, placing her hand on the doorknob. "Well, I made this turkey meatloaf and potatoes for us to enjoy tonight. We'll eat dinner at your house. Go on over and I'll bring our plates over there." Kyle opened his mouth and before he could speak, Melanie said, "Chloe's not coming over. I'll be sure of that."

Kyle rushed across the street to his temporary home. He went into the bathroom and washed his face, removing the wine that has spilled onto his skin. He then brushed his teeth, still trying to erase the taste, and the feeling of longing that had flowed through him, when the first few drops of wine had landed into his mouth.

After rinsing with mouthwash, he plopped onto the top of the closed toilet, using it as a chair, holding his head in his hand. "Oh, I need help," he whispered. His cell phone vibrated in his pocket. He removed it, pleased to see his brother Keith called. "Hi, Keith."

"Kyle? You okay?" Normally, Keith's worried tone would bother him, but, right now, he welcomed the distraction.

"I'm...no, I'm not okay. I want a drink, bad."

"What happened? Just take a deep breath and calm down."

"How did you know something was wrong?"

"I didn't. I just called to see if you'd made it to the house you rented from Melanie's cousin Dale. When you answered the phone, you sounded upset."

Kyle told him what had happened at Melanie's. He ended by saying, "Chloe needs help. I don't know why Melanie feels responsible for her cousin."

Keith sighed. "I'm sure she has a good reason. Do you feel better now that you've talked about what happened?"

Surprised, Kyle nodded, his admiration for his pastor twin brother growing daily. Talking to Keith proved to be soothing. "I feel better." He took a deep breath. "I told her I was on vacation."

"That's stretching the truth a bit."

"Well, I'm on a break for a month."

"You don't know how long you'll be on a break. Did you tell her what happened at the law firm?"

He ignored the question. "Well, I'm here for a month." He mentally sighed. No way did he want to further discuss *why* he had felt the need to leave Maryland to stay in North Carolina for a few weeks. "Thanks for talking to me, Keith."

"You're welcome. Hey, how's Melanie doing?"

Kyle bristled at Keith's caring tone, even though he knew Keith thought of Melanie as a close friend. "She looks stressed to me. I still don't understand why she moved down here to open this health food and herb store. It's a little bit weird."

"Melanie's been through a lot over the last couple of years."

"Like what?"

Keith hesitated. "She broke her engagement. She was pretty messed up when she was dating her fiancé. He was abusive to her."

Kyle blinked, startled. "He used to hit her?"

"No, not abusive like that. It was more of a mind control thing. It was pretty bad. She was miserable so she broke up with him. She said it was one of the roughest times in her life."

After Kyle rang off with his brother, he slipped the phone back into his pocket, still digesting this new information about Melanie. Awful that she'd been in an abusive relationship. She deserved better.

2

Using a broom Melanie swept shards of glass from the kitchen floor into a dustpan. Afterwards she placed the cleaning utensils into the kitchen closet and faced Chloe. "You should wear shoes in the kitchen for the next few days. I think I cleaned up all of the broken glass. I'll vacuum when I get back to make sure."

Chloe shrugged. Her brown eyes were glassy as she took another drink of wine. Melanie swiped Chloe's car keys from the table and slipped them into her pocket before grabbing the dinner plates. She didn't want her cousin to drive while intoxicated.

Chloe gripped her wine glass. "Where ya goin'?"

Melanie glared at her wayward cousin before exiting the kitchen and crossing the street to Kyle's place. When she reached his house seconds later, he opened his door. "Hi, Melanie." When he spoke, she caught the faint medicinal scent of Listerine. She wondered why he bothered to use mouthwash since they were about eat dinner.

"Hey, Kyle." She held the plates up. "I've come with our dinner."

He gestured into the house. "Come on in."

Still holding the plates, she followed him into the semi-dark house into his kitchen. The white room practically sparkled in the weak evening sunlight. Melanie wondered if Kyle had done any cooking since he'd been in town.

She set the warm plates on the table. They

sat. Her heart skittered when Kyle grasped her fingers, bowing his head. "Lord, bless this food. Thank you for this wonderful day. I'm glad to reconnect with Melanie. Please help Chloe with her problems. Amen." Oh, his strong voice caused vibrations to run through her gut all the way to her toes.

"Amen." She squeezed his hand. Holding his hand felt so good, so warm, so comforting. She reluctantly released his hand.

Taking her fork, she sliced into the meatloaf. Thick, fragrant tomato sauce covered the meat. The cubed potatoes and mixed vegetables were dotted with pepper, basil, and spices. She sniffed, loving the aroma of her meal. She sampled her meatloaf, taking extreme pleasure in the way the herbs and spices danced on her tongue.

Kyle removed a loaf of wheat bread from the counter and slathered it with butter. "Would you like some bread and butter?"

She shook her head. Bread would taste good with the meal, but, she didn't need more carbs. "I'm okay. This should be enough for me."

Kyle bit into the bread and cut a portion

of his meatloaf. He spooned the food into his mouth. "This is so good."

"Thanks." Melanie grinned. She tried not to stare at his muscled biceps while he ate. Kyle was certainly easy on the eyes and it had been a good long while since she'd been out on a date.

He ate bite after bite and soon he scraped his plate, finishing his meal in minutes. "If we were back at your house, I'd ask for seconds." He enjoyed another piece of bread with butter.

Melanie smiled. She remembered how Kyle and his brother Keith had always eaten their meals quickly, as if the food would disappear if they didn't stuff it into their mouths fast enough. "I'm glad you like it. I could go back and get the rest."

He shook his head. "Don't bother." He stood and started a pot of coffee. Soon, the aromatic, chicory scent of the hot brew filled the kitchen. Kyle filled two coffee cups with the steaming drink. He opened a cookie jar on the counter and plopped some kind of treat onto a plate. He served the coffee and, well, it looked like dessert. "Try some of my candy."

Well, this was a surprise. She stared at

the treat and sniffed. The concoction had marshmallows, chocolate, peanuts…and well, looked like there were pretzels in there, too. Each round treat was bundled together. Smelled amazing. No way could she indulge. "Looks homemade."

He chuckled. "Yeah. It is. I made it myself." He pointed to a book on the counter. "I bought a candy cookbook. When I was in rehab they made us do different activities. I learned to make candy." He then gestured toward the table. "I made up my own recipe for rocky road candy. I call them Rocky Road Dreams."

She widened her eyes. Surprising. She never figured that Kyle Baxter would have a hobby of making candy. His brother Keith was also a candymaker. "Smells amazing. Probably too many calories."

"You worry too much. Just try some. Besides it's sugar free and low on calories."

She frowned. "Are you sure?" She had to wonder if he was telling her this just to entice her to try the dessert.

"Hey, I don't lie."

She selected one of the treats and bit into it. The taste of roasted nuts, bittersweet chocolate, salty pretzels and marshmallows exploded into her mouth with decadent sweetness. "Oh my. This is delicious." Unable to resist, she gobbled two of the treats before sipping her hot coffee.

Kyle chuckled as he consumed the remaining treats on the plate. He sipped his coffee and sighed.

Sitting here with Kyle felt so warm and comforting. She kind of wanted to sit here with him all evening instead of going home to face Chloe.

He lifted his dark eyebrows and took another drink of coffee. "Melanie, you're staring at me." He softened his words with a smile and a quick wink.

She cleared her throat and finished her drink. "Sorry for staring. It's been so long since I've seen you and you look so much like Keith—" His smile dimmed when she mentioned his twin. "But you look different, too."

He stroked the rim of his coffee cup, not responding.

"So, you're going to be here for a month for vacation?"

He finished his coffee, topping off their cups. "Well, I'm not on a real vacation." He looked away and fidgeted as if he were nervous. He used to fidget like that when they were kids. It usually meant he was up to something.

"What do you mean?"

He pointed to his laptop. "I'm going to be working on a special project. If I stopped working for a month I'd go crazy."

That sounded strange. "If you didn't want to stop working then why did you go on vacation for a month? Why not just take a week off and then return to work?"

"Just felt like something that I needed to do." It was none of her business. Her questions seemed to make him uneasy. Folks had told her over the years that she asked too many questions. She thought about his sobriety, wondering if working helped him not to drink. She drained her coffee cup and glanced into the living room, eyeing several cardboard boxes stacked on the floor. "Did you need help unpacking?"

Not responding, he finished his drink, stood, and set their cups in the sink. He then gestured toward the adjoining living room. "Come on, I want to show you something."

Curious, Melanie followed. It had grown

darker since they'd arrived. He flipped the light on. "These boxes belonged to my mother."

Melanie stopped, glanced at Kyle, her mouth dropping open. "Your mother? She's been dead since you were three and you're just now going through her stuff?"

He touched her arm. "Keith and I didn't know this stuff existed. Remember my dad got sick from cancer a few of years ago and lived with Keith before he died?"

She nodded.

"Well, after he died, Keith sold my father's house and hired someone to move most of our dad's stuff in his attic. We never looked through the stuff until recently. That's when we found these boxes."

Puzzled, Melanie furrowed her brow. The clean citrus scent of Kyle's cologne teased her nose as he stood nearby. She shrugged. "You took a month off to come down here to look through your mother's boxes?"

Taking a deep breath, he sat on the leather couch and she joined him. "I've been going through a lot over the last few years. I had a drinking problem. I had a lot of personal problems and then my dad died." He paused and fidgeted. Now she was pretty sure he was hiding something. Well, it was none of her business. If he wanted to talk about it later then that was his choice. "I just need to rest for a while and I didn't want to stay back home in Annapolis. I like the beach, and I figured I could get a lot done while I'm here in North Carolina."

He gestured toward the boxes. "I've often wondered about my mother since my dad didn't talk about her much. I remember her a little bit."

"It's so sad that you never got to know your mom." She just couldn't imagine what her life would've been like if she'd not known her mom at all. The connection she had with her mom was bold and strong – but the connection with her dad had been tenuous over the years. His drinking and womanizing had wreaked havoc in their small family. Keith had often spoken about being worried about Kyle. Was it possible that Kyle not knowing his mother may have had a negative impact on his well-being? No way could she ask him a question like that. She pushed the negative thoughts out of her mind and refocused on their conversation. "You were only three when your mom died. I'm surprised that you remember her."

He shrugged. "I know. People have said it's just my imagination – nobody remembers stuff from when they were three. But I remember her and I want to find out more about her."

"You don't know anything about her?" She still found it hard to believe that he didn't know *anything.*

He shrugged. "Not much. My dad wasn't much of a talker."

"Did your mom have any relatives?"

Kyle shook his head. "Dad told us our mom had no family."

Melanie frowned. "That's weird. Did her parents die?" It was rare to hear about somebody who had no family at all. She wondered if Kyle's mom was estranged from her family and he simply was not aware of the situation.

He shrugged again. "Dad mentioned that her parents died in a car accident when she was in her twenties. That's all I know about her family. Over the last few years I've been reflecting about my life and this is one thing that's been bothering me for a while."

He looked so serious. Serious and troubled. Maybe his taking a vacation wasn't such a bad idea after all. Hopefully being in a new environment would help him. "So you haven't looked through the boxes yet?"

He shook his head. "No."

Her phone vibrated. She removed it from her pocket and glanced at the number. Chloe. Goodness, this was frustrating. Couldn't she have the luxury of visiting with a friend without being interrupted by her cousin?

"What's wrong?"

"It's Chloe. I think I need to go back home."

"Why is it your job to take care of your cousin?" His voice brimmed with annoyance.

She didn't feel like explaining the terms of the agreement she had with Chloe's dad. "It's a long story. I'll tell you about it sometime."

The next day Melanie dusted off the shelves of her health food store. She touched the bottles and thought about the health benefits for each item. Cayenne and black pepper pills could be helpful with weight loss. Ginger could help with digestion, upset stomach, and may speed up metabolism. After she'd finished scanning the shelves, she eyed her large selection of herbal teas. A good cup of lavender tea always helped her when she was stressed.

So far she'd sold several products that morning. Hopefully her profits would continue to pour into her coffers and she'd make enough money to earn a decent salary within the next few years. She certainly didn't want to be beholden to the agreement she'd made with Chloe's dad, her Uncle Larry.

She scanned the shelves again. Some of her items were low on inventory. She expected a shipment to be coming in soon. Hopefully she'd receive it within the next couple of days. The stairs creaked. Well Chloe was finally awake – two hours late. She'd not gotten up for her morning shift. She'd tried to wake her up but her cousin slept hard, snoring, refusing to get out of bed. If she'd not made an agreement with Uncle Larry then Chloe would've already been fired from her job of working in the health food store.

Still sporting her robe and slippers Chloe

slipped into the shop. "Oh, hi." she mumbled. She just couldn't respond to her cousin's lukewarm greeting as she followed her into the adjoining kitchen. The leftover coffee she'd made earlier that morning still sat in the pot. Chloe poured a cup and took a sip. She spit out the concoction. "That stuff is almost cold. Could you make a fresh pot of coffee?"

She squeezed her eyes shut and pressed her hands together. *Lord give me strength.* "Why don't *you* make the coffee?"

Chloe folded her arms in front of her chest and leaned against the kitchen counter. "I know you're mad because I got up late, but I'll make it up to you. I don't feel well this morning."

She glared at her cousin. "You don't feel well because you were up half the night drinking wine and talking on the phone to your friends. Can't you be more responsible? Uncle Larry wants you to learn to take care of yourself—"

"I don't want to talk about Dad right now."

She grabbed Chloe's shoulder, forcing her to turn around. "We'll talk about your dad because he's supporting you while you act like an ungrateful fool."

Chloe winced, shaking Melanie's hand away. "I'm going back to bed," she mumbled.

"No, you won't. You're supposed to be helping me." Her voice cracked through the kitchen like a whip.

She gasped when Chloe got into her face, her bad morning breath making her cringe. "Mel, you can't tell me what to do! You're not my boss!"

"You can't talk to me like that!" She grabbed Chloe's arm, but Chloe pulled away and pushed her before racing up the stairs. Gritting her teeth, her heart raced while she forced herself to calm down. She took a few deep breaths. She wanted her herb store to be successful. She wished Chloe would admit to her problems and get the help she so desperately needed.

Could this day get any worse? *Lord, what am I supposed to do? This store means everything to me. If I fail, I don't know what I'm going to do.*

3

Huffing, Kyle lifted the dumbbells one final time. Whew that was the end to the weight-lifting portion of his late-evening workout. He placed the weights on the mat and grabbed a bottle of water and took a long drink. The cool liquid quenched his parched throat. He guzzled the entire container of water before tossing the empty bottle into the recycle bin.

After wiping his face with a towel, he grabbed his keys, exited his temporary home and stepped outside. The slap of the waves crashing against the beach relaxed him as he locked the door and glanced across the street at Melanie's house. The shop was closed, but Melanie's car sat in the driveway. He stared at her house. Maybe he should stop by for a visit. No, he'd go for a run and then decide if he should visit later. They'd just seen each a few days ago. He didn't want to seem too pushy by showing up at her house unexpectedly.

Taking a deep breath, he planned on getting the cardiovascular part of his workout completed. He dropped the keys into the pocket of his shorts and started running. He traipsed toward the white sandy beach and ran into the direction of town. The brine of the salty air smelled enticing. A few people congregated around the beach. Some couples strolled by holding hands and a few folks traipsed by taking their dogs for a walk.

He eyed the ferry gently moving along the water. He'd been glad that the house he'd rented was on the Outer Banks mainland.

He liked that he was able to drive directly to the house from Annapolis. To travel between the islands the residents used the ferry. He figured he'd take a ferry ride sometime during his stay. Hey, maybe if he and Melanie spent more time together they could go on a ferry ride as a date or something. Since it was Sunday evening, most of the shops and restaurants on the nearby boardwalk were empty. He continued running. Seagulls dove through the sky, frequently landing on the beach, searching for stray crumbs of food.

He ran hard for a half hour before he stopped. Whew. What a hard workout. He really needed it. Breathing deeply, he thought about the Thanksgiving dinner he'd shared with Melanie a few days ago. He kept thinking about what Keith had told him about Melanie's failed engagement. Figured Melanie would confide to Keith since they were so close. Well, it was probably for the best. Keith had always been there for Melanie and he'd not been in the best shape when Melanie was going through her breakup. At the time he'd been a functioning alcoholic who was grieving over his own broken engagement.

He lifted his head toward the sky. The warmth from the sun and the sound of the waves made him feel good. His life was such a big pathetic mess. Being here at the beach made him forget his problems. He wiped the sweat from his face. If he wanted to start something with Melanie, he eventually needed to tell her everything about the past few years of his life.

He approached the boardwalk, about to trek home, when he spotted a familiar female figure hunched on a bench. The short, tight skirt and provocative blouse gave him a good view of Chloe's slim body. She clutched her phone. Tears streamed down her cheeks as she yelled into the phone. Her arms shook as her shouts rang along the shore. Several people looked her way and some stopped and whispered, pointing at the young, distraught woman.

Kyle trotted over to Chloe. He touched her shoulder. "Chloe."

She pushed his arm away, glaring. Suddenly recognition dawned in her brown eyes as she looked at him and her expression lost some of its' hostility. Sniffing, she wiped her nose with a tissue, still clutching her phone in her other hand. "Oh, hi," she mumbled.

He glanced at her phone. "You okay?"

She nodded. More tears poured down her cheeks. "I'm fine. I'm just trying to get everything straightened out here." She turned away, as if he were being dismissed.

Kyle stroked his beard. What should he do? "Did you want me to walk you home?"

Her mouth set in a tense line as she turned around and glared at him again. "No, I'm fine. Just leave me alone." Her voice lowered and it sounded like she was defeated. Her shoulders drooped as she whispered good-bye into the phone before slipping it into her pocket. Not wanting to leave her alone he sat beside her on the bench. "I told you to leave me alone," she said in a hard voice.

He gestured toward the phone she'd just slipped into her pocket. "Who was that?"

Her eyes narrowed. "None of your business." She glared at him from head to toe. "You're just like Melanie, asking me questions. I'm not a kid."

He sighed. How did Melanie live with this emotionally distraught woman? He placed his hand on her shoulder again. Hopefully he could calm her down. "Chloe, you're sitting here shaking and crying and you look a mess. You were yelling so loud that people were staring. I just want to make sure you're okay."

"I'm fine. Just leave me alone so that I can think." She pressed her forehead into her hand. Her shoulders hunched.

He removed his hand. "Why don't you let me walk you home? I promise I won't ask any more questions."

"I said no." Good grief. Her loud voice hurt his eardrum. Several people looked toward them so he scooted away from her.

"Is there a problem over here, miss?" A large, tall, beefy muscular man towered over their bench. He looked at Kyle as if he wanted to punch him in the mouth. "Is this man bothering you?"

He shook his head. What a high price to pay for trying to be helpful nowadays. "I was just leaving." He stood up and walked away. Glancing back, he was relieved when the huge man also left Chloe and sauntered off. There was no way he wanted the people in this beach community to think he was harassing Melanie's cousin.

When he arrived home he glanced across the street and saw that Melanie's car wasn't there. Too bad she was gone. He'd wanted to talk to her about Chloe's strange behavior. After showering and eating a microwaveable dinner, he sat in front of the living room window and answered a few texts. He then accessed his email. He was working with a job recruiter – seeking new opportunities. She'd pinged him while he was out running. This recruiter was aggressive. Surprising to see her working on a Sunday.

He glanced across the street again and witnessed Chloe walking to her front door. He abandoned his chore and walked to the window to get a better view. She wiped her face, still crying. She looked toward his house and caught him staring. She glared at him before entering her home, slamming the door behind her.

Melanie's alarm buzzed. Time to get up and start the day. She pulled herself out of bed and peeked into Chloe's room. Where was she? Maybe her cousin had surprised her and had gotten up on time for a change. Her heart lightened when she figured that Chloe was suddenly growing more responsible and was probably downstairs getting ready to start work.

Melanie trudged down the stairs and into the kitchen and living room. Empty. No Chloe. Where would she go so early in the morning? She glanced outside. Chloe's black sports car was not parked in the driveway. Pushing thoughts of Chloe aside, she started a pot of herbal tea. Minutes later, sitting at the table, sporting her robe and slippers, she spent a few minutes reading the news on her phone. After eating a couple of pieces of whole wheat toast coated with a thin layer of blackberry jam, she prepared for the day.

Later, she came downstairs and checked the clock. Only about an hour before the shop was scheduled to open. Chloe was nowhere in sight. Hopefully she'd not made a mistake by agreeing to her Uncle Larry's deal for opening the shop.

She pulled her box cutter from the shelf. Someone knocked on her door while she sliced open the boxes from her recent herb shipment. That was probably Chloe. Maybe she'd forgotten her key. She opened the door. Goodness. She'd not been expecting Kyle. She smiled as she looked into his gorgeous caramel brown eyes. She resisted the urge to run her fingers over his mustache and beard as her stomach dipped with pleasure. She swallowed, saying the first word that came to her befuddled mind. "Hi," she breathed.

"Hi, Melanie." He touched her face with his index finger. Her heart skittered with pleasure. She stepped back and gestured him into the kitchen.

"What brings you by?"

"Just checking on Chloe."

Melanie frowned. She sat at the kitchen table. "What do you mean?"

He straddled the kitchen chair, sitting on the seat backwards, resting his arms against the back of the chair. "I saw her yesterday evening when I was in town."

"Really? What happened?" Melanie's heart kicked into overdrive as a new thought occurred to her. "Was she drunk?" Horrified, she wondered if Chloe had been driving while intoxicated.

Kyle placed his large hand on her shoulder. The warmth from his fingers immediately calmed her down. "No, I don't think she'd been drinking." He told her what happened the previous night. "She didn't tell you about it?"

Melanie ignored his question, asking one of her own. "Did you talk to her after she yelled at you?"

He nodded. "I tried but she was starting to make a scene. She was yelling NO at me and people were staring." He then told about the large man who approached, misunderstanding the situation. "I wasn't going to start a fight with a stranger so I walked home." He then told her that he'd seen her come home. "I'd wanted to talk to you last night, but I saw that your car was gone and I didn't have your cell phone number."

"I was out visiting some of my friends. I didn't get home until midnight. When I got back Chloe was gone. I sleep pretty soundly, so I just assumed she'd gotten home late last night and I didn't hear her come in."

Kyle frowned, resting his chin in his hand. "That's weird. I wonder where she went."

Good question. "I don't know. I've never been a parent, but I now have a taste of what some parents go through when they have a teenager in their home."

Kyle glanced at the open boxes on the counter. "Did you need some help since Chloe's not here?"

She honestly didn't think Kyle wanted to help her unpack boxes but she'd accept his offer. "I'd appreciate the help if you don't mind."

He shrugged. "I've been up since five o'clock checking email and doing a bit of work. I have no plans. If you need help, I'm available."

Melanie slipped Kyle the black box cutter and he sliced the cardboard open. Glancing through the items, they companionably took the merchandise into the shop and worked together, placing bottles of vitamins and herbs on the appropriate shelves via Melanie's direction. She stepped up on a ladder as he handed her a bottle of multi-vitamins to place on the shelf. "Have you started going through your mother's stuff yet?"

Kyle nodded, lifting two more of the dark-colored bottles. "Yes."

"What'd you find?"

He stopped passing the inventory to her as

he responded. "Letters."

"Letters?"

He chuckled. He looked really cute when he smiled. "Love letters. My parents had a long-distance relationship for a while and they wrote to each other for about a year. I've been reading through those letters." He made a face. "They're kind of sappy. Makes me feel good knowing that my mother and my father were in love."

Melanie stepped down from the ladder. This sounded like something she'd like to see. She loved hearing about people falling in love. "That's so sweet. I'd like to read some of the letters one day if you don't mind sharing."

Her heart skittered when he grinned. "That'd be great."

She stacked the empty boxes and he helped her. The clean citrus scent of his cologne overpowered the unique smell of the herbs and vitamins lining the shelves. "Have you told Keith?"

His smile faded a little as she spoke of his twin. "Yes, I told him about the letters. I even read a little bit of one over the phone. He said when he has time, he'd like to sit down with me and we can look at the letters together."

She folded her arms in front of her chest. "Have you found anything else in the box besides the letters?"

He shook his head. "The letters were the first thing I found. So who knows what else is in those boxes."

Together, they opened more boxes. "I've been trying to lose a bit of weight. I've been exercising and trying to watch what I eat."

"I have some stuff that might help. It's best to take natural stuff that'll help you to lose weight." After she'd recommended some supplements for him to take, she checked her watch. "It's time to open the store."

"Okay. I'll buy these things you recommended."

"You don't have to."

"I want to. I want to see if this natural stuff really works."

She touched his shoulder. "Don't worry about paying for it. Since you're helping me out this morning until Chloe gets back, you can have the herbs for free." It appeared he was about to object but she didn't give him a chance as she marched over to the cash register and pulled the cash box from the drawer. A customer knocked on the door.

"Can you place the OPEN sign on the door and let that person in?" she requested.

He dropped his bottles onto the counter and rushed to do her bidding. He was about to unlock the shop when Melanie's sharp cry echoed throughout the store. Abandoning the door, he rushed over to her. "Kyle..."

"What's wrong?"

She gestured toward the empty cash box. "The money for the register is all gone. We had close to five hundred dollars in here and I was going to go to the bank to make a deposit today." She clamped her teeth together and closed her eyes. She forced herself not to cry. Could this day possibly get any worse?

4

I can't believe this." Melanie closed her eyes and took a deep breath. She had to calm down and figure out what to do. "Now I know why Chloe isn't here."

Kyle touched her shoulder. "You think Chloe did this?"

"Yes. I'm pretty sure." She needed to get that money back. If Chloe stole it then the theft indicated a huge problem – one that she didn't know if she could control or fix. She gritted her teeth and balled her hands into fists. The scripture about being slow to anger popped into her mind. The pastor had recited it in his sermon the previous day. *Be slow to anger...*

Lord please help me with my anger. She composed herself and managed to focus on Kyle. "I don't know for sure if she took my money, but, there's a good chance she did. That's why she was acting so funny on the beach last night. She was probably planning something that she shouldn't be doing."

The knock sounded on the door again. "Oh, I forgot the customer. I don't know if I can open the shop today."

He squeezed her shoulder. "I'll get the door. You try and pull yourself together."

He opened the front door of the shop. "Sorry we're closed right now." His voice carried into the shop, and Melanie listened, still trying to calm down.

"But I have a cold and I wanted to get some herbal tea. Your sign says you should open now." The woman coughed, and Melanie pulled herself together. She needed to help this woman if she could. She finally came to the door and smiled at her customer.

"Come on in. I'm not opening right now, but I can help you." The older woman stepped into the shop and Melanie focused on her needs. She pushed Chloe from her mind as she recommended the woman drink some Echinachea tea. The lady also purchased some herbal cough drops. "Did you want to pay by credit card?"

"I don't use credit cards. You don't take cash?" The customer sounded annoyed.

She had no change in the cash drawer. She rang up the order and was able to give the woman change scrounged from her purse. Kyle had some folded bills and change in his wallet that they were able to use to complete the purchase.

Melanie sighed with relief when the woman left. Kyle closed and locked the door. She went into the living room and sat on the couch. Kyle dropped onto the couch beside her. She placed her head into her hand. "Is there anything you want me to do?" His concerned tone cushioned the blow of the recent theft.

She turned toward him and groaned. "Yes. Give me moral support while I call Chloe's dad."

He frowned and folded his arms in front of his chest. "Chloe's dad? I'd call the police if I were you. Don't you want your money back?"

She cringed at his hostile tone. "It's not that easy."

"What do you mean?"

Despair weighed upon her so thick, she felt like a ton of bricks were pressing down on her. "Chloe's dad, my Uncle Larry, owns this shop. He used to rent it out to a local business. After Chloe's mother died, he started having more problems with her. When Chloe was much younger, we were close." She looked directly at him. "She was like a little sister to me. We would go shopping together. I'd have her over for sleepovers. I even planned her birthday party a few times because her mother was too busy."

He shrugged and stared at her. Looked like he might be trying to understand. "Just because you used to be close to Chloe doesn't give her the right to treat you like this."

She agreed. Chloe didn't have the right to treat her like this. That's why she'd been so angry earlier. "I'm not finished. My Uncle Larry knew that I had a dream of owning my own herbal shop. I also knew how hard it was to get a small business loan. He agreed to let me use this property and fund the shop as long as Chloe came as part of the deal."

Kyle frowned. "Meaning?"

"Meaning I take her under my wing and mentor her. Try to get her to be a good employee. Teach her skills that she could use at another job, or she could stay here and help me make this shop a success. She dropped out of college after her mother died and she's been nothing but trouble for Uncle Larry for the last couple of years. He says of all the people he's known, I'm the one who's had the most influence over his daughter, other than himself and her mother."

He glanced around the living room. She wondered what he thought. He was probably thinking she'd made a rotten deal with her uncle. Bright sunlight spilled through the curtains and the sound of the waves crashing upon the beach was deep and soothing. Oh, how nice it would be to leave the shop and just frolic on the beach all day. The thought of spending time with Kyle, walking along the shore, filled her mind before she mentally pushed the image away. This was not the time to think about spending time on the beach with Kyle. "Has she ever done anything like this before?"

Good question. "Of course not. If she had, I wouldn't have agreed to be responsible for her."

He glanced at the phone. "You might want to call your uncle and ask if she's ever done anything like this before. You can let him know that you don't appreciate his not being honest with you."

She reached for her phone but didn't pick it up. She dropped her hand. Had Chloe stolen before? "What makes you think she's done something like this before?"

He shrugged. "I'm pretty good at reading people. Chloe's up to something. She's got a lot of problems. I figured that from the few times I've seen her."

She shook her head. "Her mom died a few years ago and--"

"So? You and your uncle aren't doing her any favors by enabling this behavior."

"I can't talk about this anymore." She stood up. She needed to open the shop for the day and get her mind off of her cousin. She would deal with Chloe later. "I need to go down to the bank and get some money to use in the register."

He stood up. "You're still upset. Let me drive you to the bank."

She shook her head. "You don't have to."

He touched her shoulder. "I want to."

Minutes later, they were in his car, headed toward First National Bank. Neither of them spoke. She blinked away her tears. Sometimes when she was angry she cried. Such a rotten and embarrassing habit. She sniffed and glanced outside the window. Maybe if she focused on the beautiful beach her anger would go away. He stopped at a light, took one of her hands, and squeezed her fingers. "Don't cry. Everything will be okay."

"I'm *not* crying." She'd sniffed and blinked her tears away. She'd pulled herself together.

"Your shop is important to you. Chloe's taken advantage of your kindness." He released her hand and began driving when the light turned green. She again blinked away her sudden tears, suddenly enjoying a vivid childhood memory.

She was twelve years old and had spent the afternoon alone with Kyle – it was one of the rare times she'd been alone with him as a kid. Upset, she'd been crying because her parents were sending her to a special camp for overweight kids for the summer. She was leaving the following day. Kyle had listened to her and admitted that he thought she was pretty, and that her weight didn't bother him. Horrified, Melanie had rebuked his kind words and had hurt his feelings. She recalled the pained expression on his face as he'd stormed away, refusing to talk to her for the rest of the day. She'd believed that he'd pitied her and was lying about her looks. She'd always felt fat and ugly as a child and knew she wouldn't look better until she'd lost weight.

She pushed the memory away as he pulled into the parking lot of the bank. He opened her door for her and walked beside her toward the large brick structure. Such a comfort having him beside her. The glass double-doors swung open and allowed them entrance into the building. He remained in the lobby while she approached the teller's window with a withdrawal slip. She told the teller the denominations she wanted for the cash. Seconds later, the teller frowned and glanced up at her. "I'm sorry Ms. Richards. You only have fifty dollars in your account."

This couldn't be true. "There must be some mistake." The teller must've been accessing the wrong account.

Kyle approached. He touched her shoulder. "Melanie, what's wrong?"

Her heart raced. She took a deep breath and tried to calm down. "Melanie, what's wrong?" he repeated quietly.

Taking a deep breath, she relayed what the teller had said. He glanced at the young woman behind the glass window. "Could you check again, please?"

"Okay." The teller shook her head. "Only fifty dollars in this account."

"What happened to the money?" She could barely ask the question. Her hands shook she was so angry.

"If you hold on, I'll give you a print-out of the transaction activity over the last week." Minutes later the woman handed Melanie a piece of paper, folded into thirds.

He escorted her out of the building while

she clutched the piece of paper. Once they were in the car she finally made herself open it. There was only fifty dollars in the account as the teller had stated. A huge withdrawal was done a few days before. "I can't believe this is happening." Quick as she could she unzipped her purse. "Oh, where's my phone?"

He reached over and touched her hands. Electric warmth, as smooth as homespun chocolate, rushed through her. "Mel, just stop for a minute and take a deep breath. Calm down. You're so worried you might make yourself sick."

Kyle was right. She needed to calm down. After he released her hands she took several deep breaths. She needed to focus on finding her phone. *Jesus, help me.* She removed a few items from her purse before she managed to find her phone nestled at the bottom. She removed her phone and quickly accessed her bank account. "This is awful. Worse than I thought."

"What do you mean?"

"I have a checking and a savings account set up for my business. Chloe was on both of those accounts. Not only did she take out the money from my checking, she also wiped out the savings account. I had over ten thousand dollars in there."

"Mel, I'm sorry." He took her hand and squeezed her fingers. "I'll help you to straighten all of this out."

What could Kyle do? Deep breathing and moral support would not be enough to get her money back from Chloe. *Sweet Jesus. I need your help.* She squeezed her eyes shut. No, she wouldn't cry about this. Tears would do nothing to make herself feel better. She needed to take action. She just needed to decide how to do that.

5

She wanted to cry. He could tell by looking at her. The firm set of her mouth. The hunch of her shoulders. Oh, how he remembered that familiar look whenever the girls would tease her about her weight while they'd been playing on the playground. Maybe she was holding her tears in since he was sitting in the car with her. She probably thought crying was a sign of weakness and she didn't want to embarrass herself in front of him.

"I need a few minutes alone." He hesitated. Maybe it wasn't a good idea to leave her all alone right now. She looked directly at him. Her eyes sparkled with unshed tears and her hands shook. "Please."

Well, he couldn't argue with that tone of voice. He'd give her five minutes then he'd be back to see if she was okay. He opened the car door. "I'll be back in a little bit." He shut the door and strolled the boardwalk. Maybe he could buy her something to cheer her up. He spotted a confectionary. The window displayed elaborate Christmas candies. Inside the shop excited kids pointed at the chocolates. Knowing how sensitive she was about what she ate, he doubted she'd want anything sweet. But he could use some chocolate.

He strolled into the confectionary. The vivid scent of chocolate, vanilla and sweetness filled the air. *Hark The Herald Angels Sing* played from the portable speakers behind the counter. He purchased four pieces of chocolate cashew candies. He popped a piece into his mouth. The wonderful chocolate melted on his tongue. The crunchy roasted cashews tasted amazing. He continued his walk as he gobbled three pieces of the candy. He kept the fourth piece tucked into the wax paper bag. He shoved the bag into his pocket. He'd eat that last piece later.

Down the street was a florist. Maybe he could purchase her a flower. Most women loved flowers. The bell tingled as he entered the shop. The place was flooded with red roses. The scent overpowered the room. He hesitated as he scanned the flowers. The salesclerk was helping a group of customers so he took his time. He figured by the time he returned to the car Melanie would have calmed down.

He eyed a large oddly shaped flower. He sniffed the white blossom. Smelled nice.

The salesclerk approached. "That's a calla lily. It's one of our most popular flowers. Would you like to buy some?"

He nodded. "I'll take one." They returned to the register as she rang up his sale.

After he paid, she loosely wrapped the flower in white paper. "Is this for your girlfriend?" She grinned while handing him his purchase.

He shook his head. "No. It's for a friend of mine. Going through a rough time. She needs cheering up."

"Ah, well, she'll like that. Have a nice day."

He waved at the nosy salesclerk before ambling down the street. He stopped and looked at a few more shop windows. He took out his phone and checked the time. A half hour since he'd left Melanie. She should have calmed down by now and ready to go home.

He approached the car and spotted her talking on her phone. Maybe he should wait a few more minutes and give her some privacy. She made eye contact with him and put her phone into her purse a few minutes later.

He opened the car door and slid into the driver seat. "Are you okay?" Now, that was a dumb question. Of course, she wasn't okay. Since all of her money was stolen, she probably wouldn't be okay for a good long while. He inwardly winced. "Just forget I asked that question." He offered her his gift.

"I bought you something to cheer you up."

Her dark eyes were red and puffy. Yep, she'd been crying. He hated seeing a woman in tears. She hesitated before accepting it. She carefully removed the wrapping. She pressed her hands together. "My goodness."

He couldn't tell if she was excited or disappointed. Maybe getting her a flower wasn't such a good idea after all. Perhaps she thought he was getting too personal. "Kyle, how did you know?"

He shrugged. "How did I know what?"

"Calla lilies are my favorite." She lifted the flower and sniffed. The exquisite scent filled the car with luxurious sweetness. When she smiled, just a little bit, he knew he'd made the right choice. "Thank you."

"You're welcome." He'd given this a bit of thought while he'd been out walking. Before he could tell her what was on his mind, she sniffed.

"Why do you smell like chocolate?"

"I visited the confectionary. Bought some chocolate. Ate most of it. Saved a piece for later. Did you want it?"

She shook her head while fingering the flower.

"So, what are you going to do?

"I don't know. I want my money back so I have to do something. I was just talking to my girlfriends from church when you went walking. They were upset when I told them what Chloe had done."

Well, he wasn't going to hesitate about giving his advice. Sounded like Mel needed someone to give her a suggestion. "I think we need to come up with a plan."

"A plan for what?"

"We need to find Chloe and come up with a way to get your money back."

As soon as they pulled into the driveway Mel's phone buzzed. "Oh no."

"What's wrong?" After he'd proposed they come up with a plan, she'd agreed. They were going to discuss further once they'd returned to her house.

"It's Uncle Larry."

Chloe's dad.

He already knew this was not going to be

a pleasant conversation. "You want me to leave and come to your house later?"

She shook her head as she answered the call.

"Melanie, what's happened with Chloe?" Her uncle didn't sound pleased at all. His stilted, proper tone, and loud voice, added bleak sadness to an already awful day. Her uncle talked so loudly that he could hear every word, even though Melanie didn't have her phone on speaker setting.

"What do you mean?"

"You know what I mean, young lady. I've called my daughter twelve times over the last day and her phone goes straight to voicemail. She isn't responding to my texts or emails. Where is she?" He spoke his last sentence slow and extremely loud.

"Uncle Larry she's gone. She took most of the money from the shop's checking and savings accounts."

"I told you that you must make Chloe behave if you want me to continue to support your business. If my daughter isn't home by the end of the week then I'm pulling all funding from the shop."

She gasped and pressed her hands

together. This had been such a distressing day for her. He couldn't let this angry pompous man hang up on Melanie before she got an answer to her question. He touched her arm. "Ask him if she's done this before." He spoke the words quietly – hoping Melanie would ask her uncle the question before he hung up.

"Who is that?" Uncle Larry's voice boomed from the phone. "Do you have a man there? Did he spend the night? Are you being a bad influence on my daughter?"

Oh, the nerve. The urge to punch this man in the mouth consumed him. Good thing they were on the phone and not in person. He didn't think he could stomach being around such a foolish person. He gestured toward the phone. "Put it on speaker." She hesitated before doing as he requested. "Larry, I'm Kyle Baxter – a lawyer from Annapolis. My brother and I have been friends of Melanie's family for decades. I'm the person who rented the house across the street from your son Dale."

"Oh." This seemed to calm him down a little. He wasn't sure why. Might as well move forward with what he needed to know. "We were wondering if Chloe has ever done this before."

"Done what?" The pompous arrogant tone was back.

"Stolen."

"Now, listen here---"

"We believe she stole the money from the store. Melanie had her listed on the bank accounts for convenience. She took advantage of that by taking most of the money from the bank accounts. If you want to help us find her and if you're concerned then you need to tell Melanie the full extent of Chloe's problems."

Melanie narrowed her eyes and glanced at him. Her mouth set in a hard line. Oh, no. She was angry. He understood if she felt this was a family problem and she probably didn't want him sticking his nose in her business. But he wanted to help her. That's all he was trying to do.

"Yes. She's stolen before."

Her mouth dropped open. "Why didn't you tell me before?" Her voice snapped through the car like an angry whip. She clasped the phone in her hands. If he didn't know better, he'd think that she was about to use the phone as a weapon.

If she'd known the extent of Chloe's problems would she have agreed to this terrible deal in the first place?

"I didn't think you'd agree to mentor her if you knew. I thought your strong influence on her would work and she wouldn't do these things."

Okay, now they needed more details. "What's she done?" He asked the question before Melanie could.

"She's shoplifted from stores. Since it was in our area, I knew the owners of the stores and they didn't press charges."

"What? Did you pay them off with a bribe or something?" He couldn't keep the rancid tone from his voice. His actions enabled Chloe's terrible behavior. He should have punished her and held her accountable.

Larry ignored the question. "She's also smoked weed recreationally. Has done that a lot."

"Uncle Larry. You were dishonest with me. You have no right to be angry with me."

"Well, I'm funding your shop young lady. Bring Chloe home if you want to continue receiving my support."

Before anyone could say anything her uncle ended the call.

6

could have handled that myself. This isn't your problem." She certainly didn't need Kyle's help in finding Chloe.

"I was only trying to help."

"I don't need your help. I was perfectly capable of taking care of this myself."

"Maybe you need a few more minutes to cool off." Goodness. He didn't even apologize for his nosy actions. Looked like he felt that his conversation with her Uncle Larry was perfectly justified. "Why do you put up with your uncle anyway? Why is this shop so important to you?"

"It just is. Look, I'll have to talk to you later. I need to open up the shop for the day." Maybe she could manage to make a few sales. Lord knew she needed the money more than ever.

She got out of the car and slammed the door. After she'd entered her shop she stopped and sniffed. The wonderful scent of lavender, flowers and evergreen filled the air with aromatic sweetness. She plugged in her Christmas tree. Since it was the first week of December she was glad that she'd put her tree up. She could enjoy it all month. The tree lights twinkled in her shop. She flipped the sign to open. She took a deep breath. She should probably close the shop for the day, in spite of what happened, but, she just couldn't bring herself to close.

She needed to calm down. She went into her kitchen and put on a pot of water. Five minutes later she poured the steaming water over a lavender tea bag. A nice hot cup of lavender tea would make her feel better. As she sipped the brew she closed her eyes. Her deal with Uncle Larry made her feel cornered, like a caged animal with no escape. Kyle, bless his heart, had wanted to help her. In her anger, she'd pushed his helpfulness away, as if she didn't want it.

But, she did want his help. She just wasn't sure if accepting his help would be a good idea. During this brief time they'd been spending together she found that she was starting to like being around him. He was certainly easy on the eyes. His voice was so deep and hypnotic – reminded her of the semisweet chocolate she'd put into her low-fat cookies. Intelligent. He seemed to know how to handle a situation. Take charge. When was the last time someone had taken charge and given her help?

Her ex-fiancé had taken charge, but he'd not helped her. Not one bit. He'd tried to control and manipulate her. She'd been in love and her ex had treated her like a puppet on a string, coercing her to do what he wanted her to do. Because she'd been so deeply involved with him, loved him so much, she'd not been able to clearly see her ex's manipulation tactics. Her friends had tried to warn her but she'd not listened. Once she'd discovered the depth of his manipulation – her self-esteem, her dignity – had been shattered.

He'd made snide comments about her hair, her weight and physical appearance. Once he'd made a cruel comment about how she'd styled her hair. He'd told her to cut it. He kept making the same comment about her hair. Upset about it she'd cut her hair to please him. A few times she'd gone a couple of days without eating just because of something he'd said. Just thinking about those dark days made her tired. So sad and so tired.

She sipped her tea. "Lord, I really need your help right now." She finished her tea. After rinsing out the cup she took Kyle's calla lily and placed it into a tall thin vase. She put an aspirin in the vase to keep the flower fresh. She filled the vase with water. Kyle was right. She did need to come up with a plan.

Throughout the day she started her search for Chloe in between helping several customers. Using her laptop she searched through Chloe's social media accounts. There were several videos and pictures of her with a handsome young brown-skinned man. His hair was cropped short and his nose was pierced. "Why have I never seen this man before?" In several pictures the two of them kissed.

"We're getting married!" Chloe screamed the words as if there were no tomorrow. The video had been shot a few hours ago in front of a jewelry store. Her heart skipped with dread. She carefully scrolled through all of the comments, pictures and videos on all of Chloe's social media accounts. Chloe didn't give any indication about where she was located. Some of her friends asked about her current location but she responded that it was a secret.

She groaned. What was she going to do? How in the world could Chloe be engaged to a man whom Melanie had never seen before? She pressed her hands together. Goosebumps covered her arms. Why was it suddenly so cold? She grabbed her sweater and opened the door to her deck. The sky was overcast and the water wildly crashed onto the frigid beach. Shivering she closed the door. She bowed her head. *Lord, please help me to find Chloe. Amen.*

Man, it was cold outside. Kyle trudged toward his house after his late afternoon run. Earlier when Melanie had gotten mad at him for trying to help her he'd been upset. He'd stewed about it for a good long while. He'd made a huge batch of Rocky Road Dreams candy that afternoon. He made enough candy to fill the two cookie jars that were on the kitchen counter. He'd also spent some time looking through his candy cookbook. During his time off he wanted to try some new recipes. After he was done candy making he'd gone for a long run. He cupped his frigid hands against his mouth and blew into his palms trying to warm up. Goodness this was some weird weather. Thanksgiving it was so warm and now four days later it was cold as ice. From what he'd heard over the years, the Outer Banks rarely got so frigid. Nearly thirty degrees outside. He glanced across the street. Melanie's car was in her driveway. Should he go and visit her?

No. He'd let her cool off before he approached her again. He sure was worried though. How could her uncle be such a jerk? Melanie had bravely agreed to mentor Chloe and her uncle didn't even thank her for her generosity. She needed to sever her business agreement with her uncle and try to find funding elsewhere.

His stomach grumbled. He'd worked up an appetite jogging on the beach. He removed ground turkey, mozzarella and cottage cheese from the fridge. He'd been craving a pan of lasagna over the last few weeks. He halved his recipe since he was dining alone. After pulling a can of tomatoes and dried herbs, salt and pepper from the cupboard he started frying the meat. He chopped up onion and garlic. The savory delicious scent of tomatoes and spices filled the kitchen. His mouth watered as he layered cheese, noodles and meat sauce into the pan. Too bad he'd have to wait for it to bake for a half hour. He wanted to eat now.

While the lasagna baked he removed a bunch of green grapes from the fridge. He rinsed off the grapes and dumped them into a bowl. He carried the bowl of fruit into the living room. Eyeing the boxes that had belonged to his mom, he tried to decide which one he should open next. He popped a few grapes into his mouth. The cool firm grapes were sweet and tasty. He continued scrutinizing the boxes as he munched on his before-dinner snack. He'd finished reading the stack of love letters his parents had written to each other. Melanie had said she'd like to see the letters. He could imagine a woman enjoying those sappy love notes.

One of the boxes had 'research' scrawled onto the side. Hmm. He'd not noticed seeing that word on the box before. He put his grapes aside and pulled the box from the top of the stack. He opened it. Several red folders were in the box. He removed one. The oven beeped. Well he'd look at that after he ate. His stomach growled and his mouth watered.

He removed the hot pan of lasagna from the oven. Man, this smelled wonderful. He put it on the stove to cool and went over to the window. He peered over at Melanie's house. Her car was still in the driveway. He eyed the pan of lasagna before glancing at her house again. Nah, he wouldn't ask her to join him. She'd probably say no anyway. After pouring a glass of iced tea he cut a huge slice of lasagna. Melted cheese oozed onto his plate. *Lord thank you for this food. Please help Melanie with her problems. Amen.* He was too hungry to pray any longer. His stomach growled again. He sliced his fork through the pasta and took his first bite.

He moaned. Delicious. Great that Keith had shared his secret lasagna recipe with him. Keith loved to cook and now he'd discovered something that he enjoyed just as much as his twin brother. Once he'd polished off his dinner he returned to the living room and flipped through one of the red folders from the box marked research. The letterhead of a private detective agency was etched at the top of a stack of written correspondence. Whoa, his mom had hired a private detective? He continued reading through the numerous documents. The notes. His mom had even kept a journal, which was also included in the box. He removed the journal from the box. He'd look at that later. Too keyed up to sleep, he started a pot of coffee as he read through each and every piece of paper in the folder.

His heart pounded like a sledgehammer. He was finally finished reading through the box of contents just as the sun was beginning to rise. What he'd just discovered about his mom. How could he have not known this about her?

Taking a deep breath, he called his brother. Keith answered on the first ring. "Kyle, what's wrong?" Keith probably knew something was troubling him since he was calling so early.

He took several deep breaths. "Keith…"

"You okay? Are you sick?"

"No. I have something on my mind."

"What's wrong?"

"Remember when we were talking about Dad never telling us much about Mom?"

"Yeah?"

"Well one of her boxes is marked research. Inside the box are documents – reports that were given to her by a private investigator that she'd hired." He took a deep breath. "There's no easy way to say this. Our mom was adopted." He took another deep breath. "Our mom found her birth mother – our biological maternal grandmother."

7

Nothing but shocked silence. "What?" He'd never heard such disbelief in Keith's voice. "Are you sure?" It was surprising to both of them. Their mom had always been somewhat of a mystery. She'd died when they were young. Their dad rarely spoke of her. They didn't know of any living relatives.

"Yes. I'm sure. I have the name and address of her birth mother, our maternal grandmother."

More silence. He could hear Keith breathing. "I just had to sit down."

"You're surprised. I wish you were nearby. I want to sit with you in person and talk about this. Go through mom's things together."

"We'll do that soon. I promise." Both of them were silent for several minutes. "What's the name and address?" Keith spoke so softly that he could barely hear him.

"Phoebe White. 2700 Cornflower Lane. Ginger Falls Pennsylvania."

More silence. "She might not even live there anymore. Is she...is she..."

"Little brother calm down." Kyle had been calling Keith little brother for as long as he could remember. It was a nickname that Kyle had adopted for his twin since Kyle was born ten minutes before Keith. It seemed as if their roles were now being reversed. Usually Keith was the stronger one, comforting Kyle. Now it looked as if Kyle would need to do what he could to keep Keith calm. Kyle had read and digested all of this information overnight. Yeah, he was still a bit shocked but he could imagine it being worse for Keith since he'd just heard this information a few minutes ago. "You probably want to know if she's still alive."

He hesitated. "Yes. I do."

"I thoroughly researched this last night. There's no death record for Phoebe White so I assume she's still alive. She's also the registered owner for the house on Cornflower Lane."

"So, our mom met her birth mom?"

"I don't know."

"But, you just said she did all of that stuff to find her birth mom."

"Yeah, but, I don't know if she met her. Maybe she contacted her birth mom and her birth mom may have decided not to meet up with her."

He glanced at the journal that he'd put aside for later. "Mom kept a journal. I haven't read it." He paused for a few seconds. "I figured we could read it together. I just don't..."

"You don't want to finish going through her stuff by yourself. You want us to do it together because you don't want to find any more surprises by yourself. I understand."

Keith knew him so well.

After he ended the call with Keith he could barely keep his eyes open. He didn't even have enough energy to walk into the bedroom. A pillow and a red blanket rested on the left side of the couch. He laid on the pillow and covered himself with the blanket. The house was so cold. He was too tired to turn up the heat. He closed his eyes.

The pounding knock on his door startled him awake. He jerked and fell off of the narrow couch onto the hardwood floor. "Ouch." Opening his eyes, he glanced at his watch. It was one o'clock in the afternoon! He'd not meant to sleep for that long. That irritating pounding knock again. He managed to get up. Man, so cold in this house. He peered through the open window and immediately saw the overcast sky. Looked like snow was coming. Heck, it would probably be rain. It rarely snowed here.

Dang, his foot hurt. Must have landed pretty hard on that floor. He limped over to the door and opened it.

Melanie.

She looked fetching in a blue warm up

suit and sneakers. Looked like she'd just finished exercising. The urge to hug her consumed him. After what he'd discovered last night, he felt a bit uneasy and confused. He felt like he needed someone to help him sort through all of these feelings tumbling inside of him like a wild snowstorm. He'd focus on Melanie for now and think about his maternal grandmother later.

"Kyle. You look awful."

He said the first thing that popped into his mind. "I slept on the couch this morning. Didn't sleep last night." He gestured for her to come inside.

"It's freezing in here."

"Let me turn up the heat. I'll be back in a few."

After he adjusted the heat and washed up and changed he entered the kitchen. Melanie was sitting at the table holding her hands together. "Are you okay?" She asked the question tentatively, as if she were afraid of his response.

Might as well be truthful with her. "No, I'm not okay. I found out some stuff about my mom last night. But, I don't want to talk about it right now. Okay?"

"Okay." She sighed. "Did you drink last

night? You'd mentioned your sobriety." Thank goodness she didn't ask questions about his mom. She'd respected his privacy and he was glad about that. He wanted to digest the information a bit longer – maybe talk to Keith some more about it – before he talked about it with anybody else.

He shook his head. "No, I didn't drink last night but I wanted to."

"Kyle, I'm sorry."

"For what? The stuff I found out about my mom is not your fault."

She shook her head. "Not about your mom. I'm sorry about the way I acted yesterday. You were only trying to help."

"Just forget about it." It was no big deal.

"Well, if you need to talk about your mom, I'm happy to listen. No pressure."

He nodded.

She smiled. "Smells delicious in here."

He gestured toward the leftover lasagna. "I cooked last night. Have you had lunch?"

"No. I'm starved. Does the lasagna have a lot of calories?"

"No, it's low fat. I used ground turkey, low fat cheese, whole wheat pasta..." he finished listing the ingredients as he served up two servings of the lasagna. While it warmed in the microwave he retrieved the bowl of grapes he'd left in the living room the previous day. He rinsed them off. As they enjoyed their meal Melanie told him about how she'd been lurking on Chloe's social media, trying to determine where she was located. "Can you imagine her getting married? If she gets married my uncle will pull his funding right now."

He still wondered why it was so important for her to have her shop. Couldn't she just work for a few years and save up the money she needed to pursue her dreams? She'd been a bit testy with him the last time he asked about that, so he figured it best if he not ask again. Maybe she'd open up to him about that later. Well, sounded like she needed some help with finding Chloe.

Melanie washed their lunch dishes. She shooed him away when he'd offered to help. Once she was done he invited her into the living room. "You mentioned checking Chloe's social media accounts."

"Yes?"

"What about her boyfriend? Did you check his social media?"

Now, why hadn't she thought of doing that? Kyle took charge and opened his laptop. "I'm not connected with Chloe on any social media so I probably can't see all of the activity she posted."

"Log out and let me log in." After she'd logged in and showed Kyle the videos and pictures she'd been looking at the previous day, they scrolled through Chloe's list of connections. Since they knew what her boyfriend looked like, they were hoping to find him on her list of friends. "There he is." She couldn't keep the excitement from her voice. They scrolled through the activity on his wall. "Hey, why can we see all of his activity if we're not connected to him?"

Kyle shrugged. "Probably the way he has his settings." Chloe's boyfriend was named Drake. He'd recently posted a video of himself. Kyle pressed the 'play' button on the video. Drake stood in the middle of a white room and silently stared at the camera for a few seconds. Then he opened his mouth and started singing. He sang *Oh Come All Ye Faithful* acapella. It sounded so good that she turned the volume up. Once Drake was finished with the song she resisted the urge to play it again. Chloe's boyfriend had a great voice.

Melanie grabbed his arm. "That gave me goosebumps. He sounds amazing."

"Yes he does."

She excitedly shook his arm. "Look. That looks like the same thing Chloe posted yesterday."

Drake also posted a video of the two of them in front of the jewelry store. Kyle played Drake's video. He stopped the video and pointed to the jewelry store. "We can see the name of the jewelry store on Drake's video." The name of the jewelry store was Zulfer's. After a quick Google search they immediately discovered that there was only one Zulfer's Jewelry Store and it was located in Ginger Falls Pennsylvania.

Kyle jerked back and quickly stood up. He walked to the window and looked outside. Why was he acting so strange? "What's wrong?"

He shook his head. "Nothing."

Well, she knew something was wrong. He

was acting weird. She needed to remember that her and Kyle hadn't spent any time together in years and they were just reconnecting. She needed to get to know him again. Maybe he was going through some problems and she'd irritate him with her nosy questions. The urge to kiss away his frown rushed through her. She sighed. No way should she be thinking about *that* right now. They needed to find Chloe and convince her to return home. "Since Zulfer's is in Ginger Falls Pennsylvania then maybe Chloe and Drake are still there." While Kyle stood at the window she did some sleuthing online about Ginger Falls. "It's a small town. Looks like the town does a lot of decorating for Christmas. Ginger Falls has been featured in a lot of magazines because of their high level of Christmas décor."

"I wonder if there's any way for us to find out if they're still in Ginger Falls," she mumbled. She glanced at Kyle. His eyes were closed. Maybe he was praying. She wished she knew what was troubling him. Maybe she could help.

Kyle finally opened his eyes and looked toward her. "Are there any hotels in Ginger

Falls?"

She searched. "Yes. There are five of them. But if they are staying in a hotel, I doubt the hotel would tell us that information."

He returned to the couch and sat beside her. Good gracious he smelled delicious. His aftershave reminded her of fresh lime and nature. She sniffed. Reminded her of being in the middle of a grove of limes with the wind blowing. Intoxicating. "Why don't we call the hotel and ask to be connected to their room."

She frowned. "You mean call the front desk and then they'd ring the phone's land line in their room if they're staying there? Would they do that? Wouldn't they be concerned about protecting their guests' privacy?"

He shrugged. "It's worth a shot."

They called four of the hotels. They asked to be connected to Chloe's or Drake's room, using Chloe's and Drake's first and last names for clarity. They weren't able to locate them.

He pointed to the computer screen. "One more left. The Snuggle Inn."

She shivered. "Looks hideous." The Snuggle Inn looked like a scary dive where drug deals and prostitution took place. It had several one-star reviews. From what she could tell most folks stayed there because the nightly rate was cheap. "Do you really think they're staying there?"

He shrugged. "We can check. Chloe stole most of the money for your business. They might want to stay in a cheap hotel to make it last." She was about to click the Snuggle Inn's phone number to dial on her smart phone to make the call. When he placed his hand over hers, her skin warmed. Her heart skipped. "Hold on a sec."

"What's the matter?" It suddenly seemed too warm in the room. It took her a minute to realize he'd placed his hand over hers to stop her from calling the number. "You think it's a bad idea to call?"

When he removed his hand, her skin felt cold and vacant. "No, not that. I should've thought about this in the first place."

"What?"

"If Chloe *is* staying in that hotel, what do we say when we're connected to her room? She'll realize that we know where she's staying and she might run. Then we'll be back to where we are now – not knowing where she is and not sure how to approach her."

That made sense. "What should we do?"

"If the front desk connects us to the room, we'll know she's staying there. We'll hang up, and then decide what to do next."

Sounded like a good idea. "Okay." She clicked on the phone number and put the phone on speaker so that Kyle could hear. The phone rang several times. "Doesn't seem like anybody's answering. Maybe the front desk clerk went to the restroom or something."

"Hello?" A young, peppy female voice greeted them. Melanie wondered if The Snuggle Inn had changed their number. The lady didn't answer the phone as if she were manning a business.

"Is this The Snuggle Inn?" Melanie asked.

"Yes. We don't take reservations."

"I wasn't calling about a reservation. Could you ring Chloe Richard's or Drake Mitchell's room? I'm not sure which name they used when they checked in."

The girl sighed. "Ugh. Hold on." She sounded as if Melanie's request was the worse chore in the world. After several minutes a phone rang. "Kyle, she must be staying there." Her heart sped with excitement.

"Hang up. We don't want her to know that you're calling."

She hung up. "Do you think the front desk clerk will say anything to Chloe or Drake about my phone call? Won't she be able to see my number on the front desk's caller ID?"

He shrugged. "Maybe but that clerk sounded young and not very accommodating. Took her a long time to answer the phone. Nice of her to connect us to the room but I figure she probably won't mention your phone call to anybody." He typed a few things into the computer. "Let's see how far it is. Maybe we can drive over there."

"Drive? Are you kidding?" Had he not been watching the news?

"Do you want Chloe back or not?"

"Yes, driving's a good idea but what about the snow?"

"Snow? What do you mean?"

"They're expecting a big snowstorm. The closest airport has cancelled most of their flights. It's a big deal since the Outer Banks hasn't had a snowstorm in years. It might be a bad time to be on the road. They've been talking about it for all day."

He shook his head. No wonder it'd gotten so cold all of a sudden. "I haven't been keeping up with the news. How much snow are they expecting?"

"At least a foot. The snow is supposed to start at one o'clock tomorrow morning."

"If we leave soon, we should be there before one o'clock. I have a four-wheel drive. I'm not afraid to drive in snow. If it gets bad we'll pull over."

She wasn't sure if that was a good idea. What if they pulled over the side of the road and froze to death? But, she wanted Chloe back safe and sound. She wanted to call her Uncle Larry and let him know that she had everything under control. She closed her eyes and took a deep breath. She opened her eyes and looked at Kyle. She was attracted to him. Didn't sound like a good idea to be with him alone on the road for nine hours.

She searched the internet for deaths during a snowstorm.

Kyle looked over her shoulder to see what she was researching. He chuckled. "Mel, you need to calm down. We won't freeze to death."

She ignored his humor. "Looks like most of the deaths in the United States from hypothermia happened in people's homes. Their heat went out during snowstorms."

"Go and get your stuff. Meet me here as soon as you can. Do you think you'll be ready to go within an hour?"

He got up from the couch. Suddenly, it hit her. He was going to drive her through a snowstorm to get Chloe – and she'd not told him *why* her store was so important to her. She wasn't even his girlfriend. She didn't want this trip to interrupt his routine. "What about your job? You told me this was a working vacation for you."

He looked away and scratched the back of his neck. He was hiding something. A niggle of apprehension rushed through her. She ignored it. Whatever was going on in Kyle's life was none of her business. She had to keep telling herself that. "I'll be fine." He paused for a few seconds. "Look, I think the Lord wants me to go to Ginger Falls. Right now, I can't tell you why, but it's the way I feel." He took another deep breath. "I want to go for personal reasons, not just to pick up

Chloe."

"Does this have anything to do with your mom?"

He nodded. "But, like I said earlier, I can't talk about it right now." He glanced at his watch. "Let's get packed and get going before the snow starts."

8

Kyle packed his SUV with their suitcases. He then filled a cooler with ice.

"Why are you filling a cooler with ice? We're not going to the beach." Melanie stood beside him while he loaded the trunk.

She wore a thick down-filled brown coat and steel-toed Timberland boots. Although the Outer Banks seldom got frigid temperatures, she'd brought some of her winter clothing with her, just in case, when she'd relocated to the area. He also sported his thick winter coat and outdoor hiking boots. "I have the rest of the lasagna in there and several cold sodas and cold coffee drinks. I might need some caffeine to stay awake while driving." He pointed to a cardboard box in the trunk. "Your cousin Dale had some special outdoor blankets that keep you warm in cold temperatures. I found them in his closet."

Melanie nodded. "He goes on a lot of outdoor trips. He loves being out in the cold weather."

"I thought we'd take the blankets with us in case we needed them. Like I said, we should arrive before the snow starts."

She peeked into the box. "There's more in here than just blankets."

"I found some other things that we might need if it gets too cold and we get stuck. I doubt that'll happen, but you never know." He gestured toward the box. "If we use some of this stuff, I'll replace it for Dale before I go back to Annapolis."

She frowned when he mentioned returning to Annapolis. While they'd been loading the SUV it had occurred to him that in a few days' time he'd grown used to being around Melanie. While he was loading his car she'd asked him a few times about his job and if this road trip was interrupting his routine. He certainly didn't want her to know his secret.

He'd lost his job because of his drinking.

He'd gotten drunk one afternoon and then had stupidly met a client. It had been a disaster. He'd fallen off the wagon and had begun going to go to his AA meetings again. Life had been tough. When his AA sponsor had gotten sick with cancer and then died, Kyle had lost it. He'd gotten drunk, upset that his friend Earl was now gone. His one slip up had cost him his job, and now he was looking for someplace else to work. He'd wondered about setting up his own practice somewhere. That was a possibility.

"Kyle?" Melanie waved her hand in front of his face. "What's wrong? You looked like you were a million miles away."

"Just thinking is all. Don't worry about me. My going on this trip is not messing up my work schedule. Stop asking me about it."

"Okay..." she held her hands up as if defeated. "You look upset – like something is on your mind."

Once the car was packed she got into the vehicle on the passenger side. They'd decided that he would drive and she could take over if she wanted to later. She'd admitted to not liking driving in the snow, and he didn't blame her. They didn't get a whole lot of snow in Annapolis and some folks they knew refused to drive when it snowed since they weren't used to driving on slippery roads. He opened the driver's side door. "Hey, give me a few minutes. There's something I have to do, then we'll be on our way."

She nodded at him before he slammed the car door shut. He returned to the house and pulled out his phone.

He called Keith. His twin brother answered after the first ring. "You okay, Kyle?"

He sighed. "Yeah. Keith, so much has happened since I talked to you this morning." He outlined all that had happened since they'd spoken earlier. "So, I'm going to Ginger Falls because I think God wants me to."

Keith was quiet for several seconds. "That's weird. First you tell me that mom's mother lives in Ginger Falls and now you tell me that Chloe is there. It's almost as if...."

Kyle nodded. "Exactly. I figure you're going to say it's a God thing."

"Yeah. It's not as if Ginger Falls is a big city like Chicago or New York. It's a small town. I looked it up after I talked to you on the phone this morning." He paused for a few seconds. "Are you going to...meet our grandmother. Try to meet her?"

"No. It's best if she wants to meet that we'll do that together."

"I agree."

He took a deep breath. "I'm not sure why I'm going or what I'll do once I get there. I have to help Melanie find Chloe. I'll call you once we get there."

"Be careful. I heard about the snowstorm coming. It's been on national news." Before Kyle could respond, Keith continued. "Lord, please be with Kyle and Melanie. Please keep them safe. Amen."

"Amen." Kyle whispered the words.

"Did you tell Melanie about our

grandmother?"

"No. I didn't want to. It's all so new and...I don't know. Did you want me to tell her about it?"

"No. Melanie and I are close but, this is something that should just be between us for now."

"Yeah, I figured you'd feel that way." Both of them were quiet for a few minutes. "Look, I'm texting you the route we're taking to Ginger Falls. I did some research. If you're driving in a snowstorm then it's best if I tell someone the route we're taking, just in case we get lost, or, stuck in the snow. That way, they'll know where to send someone to search if we can't be found."

"Okay. Keep me posted while you're on the road."

"I will."

After he ended the call and sent the text to his twin brother he exited the house and locked the front door. Melanie relaxed in the front seat. Her eyes were closed. "You alright?"

She nodded. "Yes. I'm fine. Just relaxing."

"I had to make a phone call before we left. Hopefully we'll be in Ginger Falls before the snow starts." He drove away and took the main road to Walmart. He pulled into the crowded parking lot. Flocks of people were in the parking lot and in the store. Probably stocking up on supplies that they might need during the snowstorm.

"Why are we stopping here? I thought you wanted to get on the road." She didn't sound happy at all.

"Just give me a few minutes. Won't take me long. Did you need anything?"

"No. I want to get going as you suggested."

He sighed. "I said I'll be quick."

"But the store is crowded…"

"I'll go through self-checkout." He hurried into the store before she could object any further. He needed to make sure they had everything they needed in case they got stuck in the snowstorm. Throngs of people clamored all over the store. Looked like this was a bad idea after all. Figures. All of the bottled water was gone. Earlier, he'd found three empty water jugs with Dale's camping equipment. He'd filled them with filtered water and had them in the trunk with some paper cups. He threw some containers of nuts and a few boxes of granola cereal into his basket. He'd wanted to get them some granola bars but the store didn't have any left. He then found some chips and some peanut butter crackers.

A young pregnant woman with a toddler in her cart walked past him. The stench of feces and urine screamed from the cart. Phew. Smelled like the kid needed his diaper changed. The short, petite woman struggled to reach one of the few remaining cans of juice on the top shelf. He quickly came over to her. "How many you need?"

"Three." He lifted the gallon jugs of juice into the cart.

"Thank you."

"Need me to help with anything else?" The woman had circles under her eyes. Looked like she needed a good night's sleep.

She gripped the handle of her cart. "I need to get some diapers. Don't know if I have enough money to pay for 'em."

"You got the rest of the stuff you need?"

She nodded. He beckoned her over to the baby section. She selected her diapers. He dumped two large packages of diapers into the cart.

The young woman got into the self-checkout and he stood behind her. "I'll spot you if you don't have enough money."

She turned toward him as tears glistened in her eyes. She quickly blinked her tears away. The stench from the woman's kid was nauseating. They stood in the crowded line for forty-five minutes. Finally, it was their turn. After she'd rung up her groceries she was twenty dollars short. Kyle slid the needed twenty dollars into the self-checkout machine. She nodded toward him. "Thank you. Merry Christmas."

He nodded back. "You're welcome. Merry Christmas." The woman quickly left. Kyle rang up his items and paid with his credit card. There were no plastic grocery bags in the self-checkout. So, he placed the items back into his cart and pushed his loaded cart back out to his car.

"Took you long enough." Melanie sounded beyond irritated.

"Calm down. We need to be sure we're prepared." He loaded the items into the trunk and returned the cart. He then got into the car and started the engine. "Here we go. Maybe we'll get there before the snow starts and we can bring Chloe home before tomorrow."

Melanie gave him a sideways look. "Look,

Kyle. I'm sorry for snapping at you. I really appreciate all that you're doing for me. I'm just anxious to get on the road and find Chloe."

"Yeah, I hear you. Well, we're finally on our way." He turned some Christmas music on the stereo. They drove past the enormous Christmas tree in the downtown square as they headed toward the highway.

9

The lights from the police car glowed amidst the powdery white snow cascading from the sky. Kyle gently tapped the brake of his SUV as he came to a complete stop beside the squad car. The snow had started hours earlier than predicted. Kyle had been complaining about visibility problems for the past half hour. The snow had been getting worse and they'd agreed that they'd take the next exit to see if they could find a hotel room someplace. The policeman approached their vehicle. "Sir, we're in a state of emergency because of the snow. You'll need to get off the road as soon as you can."

Kyle nodded. "Okay, officer. We're pulling off on the next exit."

She pulled out her phone. "It's six thirty. We're barely a quarter of the way there because of the snow."

"I hope we can find a room someplace."

"I was afraid this was going to happen."

"Melanie, where's your faith? We'll be fine. We have the blankets. We can stay in the car if we have to."

"I guess you're right. I'm just being cautious."

He patted her hand. "Yeah, I know."

They took the next exit. The first thing they saw on the side of the road were signs for hotels. Kyle stopped at the first hotel. It was a cheap motel. Thankfully someone was at the front desk. As quick as they could they exited the car. The wind tossed snow all around them. The snow flying in her face felt like pricks of ice against her skin. Kyle held her hand as they scurried inside. The desk clerk had bushy gray hair and round, wire-rimmed glasses. His eyes were bleary as he got out of his seat and limped over to the counter. "Can I help you?"

Melanie took charge. "We need two rooms."

"Only got one."

"Just one?"

"Yep."

"Melanie, you can have the room. I'll stay in the car."

"We're both tired. Let's take the room. It'll be okay."

He widened his eyes and backed away from her. "You may be okay, but I won't." He gestured toward a tattered couch in the corner. "I can stay right there." He actually looked scared to death to stay in the room with her.

She sighed. "Look, just come in the room. If you need to leave, or after awhile, if you think it's not a good idea, you can return to the lobby."

He backed away from her and scratched

the back of his neck. He was obviously thinking about what she'd just proposed. "Okay."

The desk clerk gave them their key and Kyle gave his credit card to pay for the room. "Kyle, you don't need to pay for the room."

"Don't worry about it." By the tense set of his mouth, she could tell that he was angry. Maybe she should've told him to stay in the car after all. But, if he stayed in the car, she'd not be able to sleep. She'd feel guilty about having a nice warm bed to sleep in while Kyle was out in the stormy cold weather.

The room was only a few feet away from the hotel lobby. Melanie unlocked the door and entered the room. A rank odor spilled from the bathroom. "Ugh. It stinks in here."

He patted her shoulder. "Sit on the chair. I'll bring our stuff in." Several minutes later he'd unloaded their suitcases as well as the cooler with the drinks and food. Thankfully, the room had a microwave. Kyle went into the bathroom and flushed the toilet. The scent of Lysol soon filled the room. A rank odor came from the sink. The sink didn't have a stopper and when you looked down the drain dirty nasty water puddled in the rusted sink pipe. Kyle ran the water for a few minutes and then turned it off. He did this for several minutes. She frowned. "What are you doing?"

"I'm seeing if the sink is stopped up. Looks like the sink is just slow, not completely stopped up." He sprayed Lysol down the sink's hole to get rid of the nasty odor.

"I'm going to lie down for a minute." Thankfully the room had two double beds.

"No." Kyle looked mortified as he came over to the beds. "Just sit in the chair for now." He removed the sheets. She cringed when she spotted dots of blood and other stains on the sheets. He carefully scrutinized the mattresses.

"What are you doing?"

"Looking for bedbugs."

"Ugh. You think there's bedbugs in here?"

"Gee, Melanie. Of course, there might be bed bugs. This place is filthy. You were complaining about the odor as soon as we stepped into the room."

Once he was finished scrutinizing the mattresses, he nodded. "We're good. No bedbugs. I researched staying in cheap motels before we left. The article told how to check for bedbugs when staying at places like this."

Great that Kyle thought of everything. He opened the cooler and she saw that he'd even bought paper plates and plastic cutlery. They finished off the lasagna and drank cups of cold water from the gallon jugs he'd bought. He pulled a large plastic container out of his suitcase.

"You brought your Rocky Road Dreams."

She couldn't help but be excited. This low-calorie candy tasted so good.

"Yep. Recently made a fresh batch." He feasted on four pieces of candy. She slowly devoured one piece. Unable to resist she ate another one. The salty semisweet chocolate taste blended well with the marshmallows. She drank more cold water to wash down her dessert.

They took turns using the bathroom and shower. The room was so cold. She opted to sleep in her sweatpants and sweatshirt. Kyle did the same. After they were in their separate beds, it was still early evening. He got up and opened the curtains. The small parking lot was covered in an exquisite white blanket of snow.

"It's so pretty out there."

He nodded. "Sure is."

He turned the TV onto the local news. The newscaster was giving information about the snowstorm. The volume was on low. He looked pensive, as if something was on his mind. She figured he kept the volume down since he thought she'd be falling asleep. "Hey, Mel?"

"Yeah?"

"I was wondering about you, your Uncle Larry, Chloe...everything."

"What do you mean?"

"*Why* are we doing all of this to get Chloe to come home? You're relying on your uncle for funding but I don't understand *why*?"

She inwardly groaned. Hadn't they already discussed this? "I told you that funding a small business is hard. Hard to get a business loan."

"But *why* is the store so important to you. Seems like you could come up with another plan. Can't you sell your vitamins and herbs online? Keep the stuff at your apartment or wherever you choose to live if you lost the store?"

"I enjoy the face-to-face contact with the customer. Being around someone that's knowledgeable about holistic medicine is what helped me."

He frowned. "What do you mean?"

"When I was a kid, remember when my parents sent me to a camp for overweight kids?"

That was the first time Kyle had told her that she was beautiful. She'd been a pudgy kid, finding solace by eating sweets and junk food. Keith and Kyle had stopped by her house to say goodbye before she left. Kyle had hugged her and she'd pushed him away. At the time, she'd thought that he'd said she was beautiful just to make her feel good about herself. She didn't think that he really meant what he'd said.

He didn't say anything for a long time. She was starting to wonder if he was even listening to her. "Yeah, I remember." He paused for a few seconds. "What's that got to do with Chloe and your Uncle Larry?"

"I haven't finished explaining. The summer I went to that camp, it changed my entire world. The counselors were terrific and they taught us healthy eating tips that I'd not seen elsewhere. They talked about herbs and vitamins and about how we could cure our cravings by eating low-fat low-calorie foods. They also taught us about being emotionally well. Kyle, I learned *why* I was eating so much. My parents…well…they argued all the time. It was pretty bad. I thought…well, I thought maybe they were arguing about me."

"Did they mention you when they are arguing?"

"Not always. Sometimes I'd come in the middle of an argument, not knowing the entire reason why they were fighting. My mom was always on me about my weight. My dad always seemed to have his mind on something…something other than me. He let my mom do whatever she wanted when it came to caring for me. When I was at the camp, the counselors made me see that my problems didn't start with the food. They started elsewhere." She shrugged. "I like talking to people one on one, caring for them if I can. That's hard to do with an online store. I've interacted a lot with customers. I enjoy it. You might not have noticed it since you're not in the shop with me each day."

He didn't say anything for a good long while. She peeked over at him. He stared at the television, but she could tell that he was bothered. She wasn't sure if she'd responded to his question fully. "When you said your parents were arguing, what were they arguing about?"

"Well, they fussed about my weight – but I don't believe that's what was most upsetting to them. My dad had a drinking problem."

Kyle frowned and looked directly at her. "I didn't know that."

"Yeah, it's not something that I broadcasted. I think I may have told your brother about it once." He looked upset when she mentioned his twin. It was no secret that she used to have a huge crush on Keith. "Anyway, we had some financial problems a few times. My dad lost his job because of his drinking. Kyle it was so awful. The private school that I attended had called our house because my tuition had not been paid. My dad took care of all of the bills and it was upsetting to my mom when he messed up. When her friends somehow found out about our problems, my mom freaked out. She liked to put on airs and I found it highly sickening. My mom wanted everybody to think that we were this perfect family – and we were far from being perfect." She took a deep breath as she stared at the television.

"That's why I couldn't go to them for help with my store. When I'd decided to go into business for myself, and couldn't get a business loan, I knew my parents would not have been able to help. They still struggle to make ends meet because of my dad. They're close to retirement age, so, you figure they'd have straightened out their lives by now."

She took another deep breath. "But I'm a grown woman and they're not obligated to help me pursue my dreams. Anyway, my dad had mentioned to his brother, my Uncle Larry, that I wanted to go into business for myself. Uncle Larry was having problems with Chloe and he approached me with his idea. I jumped at the chance because I wanted to start my own business *now*. I didn't want to wait and seek out other alternatives. I honestly don't know if I can salvage the situation, but, at least I can try."

He didn't respond. He stared at the television and soon his deep, even breathing filled the small hotel room. She eyed him while he slept. She wondered what he thought about what she'd just revealed. She seldom told anybody about the problems she'd had with her messed-up family.

10

Kyle opened his eyes. They'd slept with one of the lamps on. He opened the curtains. The vast blanket of white was the first thing he spotted outside the window. Man, that sure was pretty. He remembered when he and Keith used to go outside to play in the snow when they were kids. They'd make snow angels. He closed his eyes tight and tried to squeeze one of the few memories he had of his mom from this brain.

His mother was a pretty brown-skinned woman with a voice like bells. She'd taken him and Keith outside to play in the snow. She'd sang a song to them, some tune about a snowman, while they'd picked up the snow. They'd tried to eat the snow and she told them not to. He opened his eyes. He *knew* his mom had taken them out in the snow. He remembered the snippet so vividly. He'd probably only been two and a half or three, but he just remembered those few minutes of his life with his mom.

He sighed. Maybe more memories would come to him if he went through the rest of her stuff. The address on Cornflower Lane still haunted his mind. What would he do when he arrived in Ginger Falls? After he helped Melanie with Chloe what was he supposed to do about his grandmother? He shook the thought away. *Lord, help me to figure out what to do. Amen.*

He glanced over at Melanie. She looked lovely. Her hair was covered with a blue sleeping bonnet. Her skin was so smooth and pretty, like rich smooth cocoa. He swallowed. The room suddenly seemed too cramped and warm in spite of the frigid temperatures outside. As quietly as he could he got out of bed and washed up. He put on his snow boots and coat and opened the door and stepped outside.

Soft gentle snowflakes tumbled from the sky like spun sugar. The snow wasn't as wild as the previous day and it appeared that it would stop soon. At least two feet of snow covered the parking lot. He entered the lobby. The old man who was at the front desk the previous evening was no longer there. Instead, a younger gentleman sat at the desk drinking a cup of coffee. The man nodded toward him. "Morning. There's coffee and donuts over there. Trying to get a snow plow to come through but they probably won't be here until tomorrow."

"Thanks." He took a paper cup and filled it with coffee. He added sugar and powdered creamer. He sat at one of the round tables and stared at the TV as he consumed four glazed donuts. As the newscaster told about the snowfall in the area and mentioned closings for schools he thought about what Melanie had revealed to him the previous night.

So, her dad had a drinking problem and he'd lost his job because of it. Melanie obviously had emotional scars because of her dad. He blew air through his lips. He felt like a failure. If Melanie knew that he was unemployed for the exact same reason as her dad was, she'd never want to go out with him – never consider having a relationship with him, if she knew. Whew. Should he come clean and just tell her everything now? If he did, she'd have time to digest this information about him. She might see that at least he was trying to make his life better. After all, he was saved and relied on Jesus. That counted for something, didn't it?

But if he told her now, she might be disgusted with him. Then she'd be forced to be in close proximity with him tonight and all day tomorrow as they made their way toward Ginger Falls. It'd be uneasy if she had strong negative feelings towards him while they completed their trip. No, he wouldn't tell her his secret now. Maybe once they found Chloe and figured out what they were going to do about her, and had returned to the Outer Banks, then he'd tell her—

Something dropped onto his shoulder. He jumped and knocked over his coffee. A puddle of brown liquid spilled onto the floor.

"Kyle, why're you so jumpy?" Melanie grinned as she quickly took napkins and sopped up the mess he'd made. She'd clapped her hand onto his shoulder earlier – he'd not been expecting her to do that.

"Don't sneak up on me like that." His came out harsh.

She frowned and threw away the soggy napkins. She then took a wad of napkins and wet them at the sink. She made sure all of the spilled coffee was mopped up from the floor and the table. A few other guests strolled in and helped themselves to the meager continental breakfast.

She got a cup of coffee and sat beside him. "What's wrong?"

"Nothing that I want to talk about."

"Didn't you sleep well last night?" He didn't respond to her question.

She touched his hand. She didn't move her hand until he looked directly at her. "Well, maybe if you talked about what's bothering you then you'd feel better."

"I told you I can't talk about it now."

She quickly moved her hand away. Her beautiful mouth pouted before she sipped her coffee. He'd hurt her feelings. Well, it couldn't be helped. "Look, I'm going through some stuff right now. I've been talking to Keith about it."

She nodded. "Your brother is one of the kindest people I've ever known. I'm sure talking to him will make you feel better." Hard to ignore the warmth in her voice when she spoke of his twin brother. Even though Keith was married with two children – he had to wonder if Melanie still liked him. It was no surprise that they stopped spending so much time together after he got engaged.

Well, looked like both of them had a lot to deal with. They needed to do something to lighten their moods. Once she was done with her coffee he pointed outside. "Let's have a snowball fight."

Melanie packed the snow in her red-gloved hands. She threw the ball at Kyle, smacking him right on his nose.

"Hey, I'm going to get you for that!"

"No, you won't." She grinned as he threw the snowball toward her. She ducked just in time. She then packed another snowball and threw it at Kyle, hitting him in the back of the head.

"I'm going to get you for that." His voice boomed in the cold frigid morning. White puffs of air came out of his mouth when he spoke. When he laughed his brown eyes twinkled. Snow had gotten stuck in his beard.

She laughed. "You look like Santa Claus."

He chuckled. Oh, when Kyle wasn't so serious, he became even more attractive. She threw another snowball and hit him on his face. "I said I'd get you for that..." When he started running on the snow packed path she realized he was trying to capture her. She turned and screamed running in the opposite direction. When Kyle caught up with her and grabbed her around the waist, they tumbled into the fresh snowbank. Both of them laughed as his face came closer to hers. Slowly his smile faded as she noticed, for the first time, he had a tiny mole right beside his left ear. His mouth was slightly open and she noticed his perfect white teeth.

He smelled terrific, like citrus and evergreen. In spite of the frigid temperatures, she felt warm and snuggly. When his mouth came closer to hers, she wasn't sure what to do. He pressed his lips to hers.

When she moaned he jumped up as if he'd been burned. "Melanie. I'm so sorry. I didn't mean..."

He didn't mean what? He didn't mean to kiss her? He turned away for a few seconds. "Kyle it's okay. Both of us are feeling a bit off. We're stuck at this lousy hotel in the middle of a snowstorm. I'm probably about to lose my business. You're kind to come along and help me out." The kiss was obviously not supposed to have happened. He just got caught up in the moment and had made a mistake. She was almost sure he felt that way. That's probably why he looked so embarrassed.

"Yeah, I guess you're right."

She didn't feel like continuing their snowball fight. Goodness, she was tired. She yawned. It'd been years since she'd played so hard in the snow. They returned to their room. She took her time in the bathroom removing her wet snow clothes and changing into her sweat suit. Her stomach rumbled with hunger. The restaurants nearby were closed because of the snow. Kyle had brought lots of snack food. She honed in on the box of granola cereal. She filled up on granola and drank a can of diet cola. She enjoyed two more pieces of Rocky Road Dreams candy. Kyle turned the TV on while he munched on snacks and drank one of the cold coffee beverages he'd bought along for the trip. He also had a few pieces of candy.

She laid down to rest for a few minutes. When she opened her eyes she was shocked to see it was going on two o'clock in the afternoon. She'd not meant to sleep that long. She glanced around the empty room. Where was Kyle?

Kyle ended the call. He'd just spoken to a recruiter about a possible job lead. He'd discovered that most companies were not going to be hiring until the new year, and he was fine with that since he'd wanted to be on vacation until the first of the year. The recruiter said some of the firms had some specific questions about his work and about the type of job he was seeking. After talking to the recruiter for an hour he'd gotten off of the phone.

He sat in his SUV. He'd not wanted to take the call in the lobby because he didn't want Melanie to come looking for him and possibly overhear him talking to a recruiter. She might ask why he was unemployed. That was a discussion he wanted to avoid for now. He blew air through his lips. Man, how in the world was he going to be able to spend the night in the room with Melanie? After that amazing kiss...

Wow. Melanie tasted as good as she looked. Her lips were soft and firm at the same time. Her brown eyes were so pretty...Ugh. He cracked the window. He suddenly felt hot. No way did he want to go back into that hotel room. The whole situation was beyond awkward. Yeah, he thought Melanie enjoyed the kiss just as much as he. But, now things seemed weird and complicated. Before the kiss they were just two friends and he was helping her out. And now?

Well, she said that both of them were a bit off right now...with the snowstorm and the personal problems each of them were dealing with...so, maybe within the next few days, they'd forget all about the fact that they'd locked lips while tumbling in the snow. After they'd retrieved Chloe and returned to the Outer Banks, things would go back to normal for the both of them. Besides he was seeking a job in Annapolis so if her Uncle Larry continued to support her business, and if she got Chloe to cooperate then they'd be living far apart. Too far apart to consider dating or attempting to have a relationship.

So awkward. How was he going to go back into that room since they'd shared such an amazing kiss? He got out of his vehicle and entered the hotel lobby. After poking around a bit, he found an empty room not far from the lobby. The room had one long table and several chairs. Looked like it may be a meeting room. From the dust on the table, looked like it hadn't been used in a long while. He found a vending machine and purchased a few packs of nuts and a cinnamon roll. He also got a soda. After he ate his meager meal his phone buzzed with a text.

Where are you?

Melanie. He just could not be alone with her the rest of the day and all night. He texted back. *Some stuff came up for work. Gotta take care of some things. In a vacant workroom at our hotel.*

11

The opening door startled Melanie awake. She opened her eyes. In the darkness she spotted Kyle quietly coming into the room. He went into the bathroom and eased the door shut. She blinked rapidly and focused on the red digital display of the clock beside her bed. One o'clock in the morning. Had he been gone dealing with a crisis at his job for this long? When the bathroom door eased open she quickly shut her eyes. She feigned sleep while he slipped into his bed.

He was obviously avoiding her because of the kiss. She was sure of it. But, he couldn't avoid her for long. They still had to drive the rest of the way to Ginger Falls. Drive in his car together, alone. She was sure the rest of the trip would be very interesting.

The following morning when she woke up Kyle was already gone. She scanned the room and noticed that all of his stuff – his suitcase and toiletries – were not in the room. She wondered if he'd gone to check to see if there was a place for them to get breakfast. They'd eaten all of the granola cereal but they still had snacks left. She yawned. He'd probably gone to get donuts and coffee. She was about to text him when the door opened and he came into the room.

He looked wonderful.

He sported jeans and Timberland hiking boots. He wore a white turtleneck under a red sweater. Looked like he'd trimmed his sexy beard. He resembled a cute, irresistible lumberjack. All he needed was an ax to chop down a Christmas tree. Her mouth suddenly felt dry and her palms grew moist. She swallowed. Maybe she'd not been drinking enough water. It took her a minute to find her voice. "Hey."

He smiled. "Hi. Look, I was talking to the front desk. The roads have been cleared. We still need to drive carefully though. Might be some slippery spots on the highway."

"Where's your stuff?"

"I already loaded the car with my things. I'm going to wait in the car. Call or text me when you've got your stuff together so we can leave."

She cleared her throat. "Did you want me to drive?"

He shook his head. "I'd better drive. You told me that driving in the snow makes you nervous."

He left before she could reply.

Fast as she could she washed up and got dressed. She then gathered all of her things and texted him that she was ready. They then loaded all of her baggage into the trunk. He drove and slowly exited the hotel parking lot via the snowy pathway.

Ginger Falls – 50 miles. Seeing the sign on the highway made him smile. Finally, they were almost there. Since they'd left the hotel Melanie had been quiet. He'd played some Christmas music on the stereo and they'd stopped for lunch. He'd eaten a burger and fries and Melanie had eaten a chef's salad and a diet soda. It was so good to eat some decent food. Melanie had insisted on treating him to lunch since he'd done all of the driving. "It's the least I can do," she'd said.

She'd also asked him about her paying him for the gas. They'd not discussed that before they left. He'd not felt like talking about her giving him money for gas. "We can talk about that when we return to the Outer Banks."

She seemed to be okay with that. He noticed since they'd gotten closer to Ginger Falls, Mel had been pressing her hands together. Her beautiful mouth was set in a firm line. She was getting nervous, probably trying to decide how to handle Chloe once they found her. "Mel, calm down. You look upset."

"I hope she's still at The Snuggle Inn. What if her and Drake have already left?"

He gave her a quick sideways look. She really did look worried. She pressed her hands together and her shoulders shook. "Stop worrying." He reached over and briefly touched her back. "You'll make yourself sick if you keep worrying like that. Pray about it."

When he glanced over at her again, her eyes were closed. She leaned her head back and kept her eyes closed while they made their way closer to Ginger Falls. When her lips moved, he figured she was asking Jesus for help.

Jesus, Melanie is not the only one who needs help. Help me. My life is such a mess right now. Amen.

He finally exited the highway onto the Ginger Falls exit. Looked like this area in Pennsylvania also got a lot of snow. The snow packed streets were not totally clear, so he had to be careful as he drove through the icy streets. Christmas lights decorated the streetlights and the stores. They slowly drove past a huge pine tree in the center of town. A sign announced a Christmas tree lighting later in the week. A salt truck drove in front of them. As the salt shot from the truck it hit the street, sounding like pebbles bouncing against the ice.

His heart skipped with joy when he spotted The Snuggle Inn ahead on their left. Since it was getting dark the motel had the name of the inn lit up on a wide sign. The T in 'the' and one of the g's in 'Snuggle' were missing from the sign. The bulbs for those letters had burnt out. He pulled into the parking lot and parked at a spot near the entrance. Melanie opened her eyes.

She looked terrified.

"Honey, calm down."

As soon as the endearment rolled off of his tongue, she whipped her head around and glared at him. "Don't call me Honey."

"Sorry." The urge to wrap her in his arms and protect her consumed him. Goodness, it would be hard to leave her when his vacation was over. He couldn't think about that right now, though. He needed to focus on what they had to accomplish right now. Chloe. They needed to find her.

"How are we going to find Chloe?"

He eyed the front desk. "Maybe I can tell the desk clerk that I'm a lawyer and I need to speak to Chloe. Maybe she'll get her on the phone – or better yet – tell me her room number."

Her mouth dropped open. "Do you really think she'll tell you the room number?"

He shrugged. They didn't have a whole lot of options. He didn't think it was a good idea for them to sit in the parking lot and wait to see if or when they spotted her cousin. Melanie grabbed his arm. "Kyle."

"What's wrong?"

She gestured toward the soda machine near the lobby. A young, brown-skinned man purchased two beverages. "That's Drake," she whispered.

"You're right."

They watched him as he grabbed the sodas and then sauntered down the snowy sidewalk. They spotted the door he'd entered. Kyle pulled out of his space and drove past the door that Drake had entered. "Looks like they're still here. Room number three."

What were they going to do? Melanie and Kyle now stood in front of the door to room three. Before approaching the door they'd been sitting in the car for an hour contemplating what to do. Drake yelled. "I'm tired of this—" he cursed. Then a loud crash resounded from the room. Deep sobs spilled through the door. Chloe.

"I can't let him hurt her." Before Kyle could say anything Melanie turned the doorknob – surprisingly it was unlocked – and rushed into the room. "Chloe." Tears rushed from her eyes when she spotted Chloe in the corner, sobbing.

She looked awful.

She had a black eye and her hands were shaking.

Drake's mouth dropped open when he spotted Kyle. He turned to swing at Kyle but Kyle ducked and Drake's fist pounded into the wall. Drake cursed as spittle ran down the side of his mouth. He was probably stoned on drugs. He ran toward Kyle, trying to grab him, but Kyle quickly moved out of the way as Drake slammed his head into the wall. Melanie grabbed Chloe's hand and thankfully her cousin didn't object. The three of them shut the door and rushed to

Kyle's car. As soon as they were inside the vehicle Kyle drove away. Drake came out of the room cursing, staring at them while they drove away, raising his fists into the air. Kyle drove several miles before parking at a nearby building. She figured he wanted to assess where they would go next, and what they needed to do. Melanie took out her phone.

"Who are you calling?" Chloe's voice sounded hoarse.

"I'm calling the police."

"No." Chloe's voice snapped through the car like an angry whip. "No police. I don't want Daddy to know."

Kyle snapped his head around to stare at Chloe in the backseat. "In Ginger Falls? Chloe, your dad doesn't even live here. He can't do anything to keep the truth from bleeding into your community. I doubt he'd find out since the crime happened here anyway."

Chloe narrowed her eyes at Kyle. "There's no crime. Besides this is none of your business. Just shut up."

Was she seriously going to talk to Kyle like that? "Chloe, apologize to Kyle, now."

Melanie raised her voice and spoke to Chloe as if she were a five-year-old child.

She lowered her head. "Sorry." The single word barely slid from her lips.

He continued to eye Chloe. "Chloe." His voice softened. "There has been a crime. You have a black eye. Did he hit you? He was yelling and screaming like a crazy person. Is he on drugs?"

Chloe mashed her lips together and eyed both of them. Tears slid down her cheeks. She pressed her hands together. "No, please don't call the police." Her shoulders shook as she cried. Melanie quickly got out of the vehicle and got into the back seat. Chloe shook as she squeezed her hands together. She screamed. Frightened Melanie didn't know what to do. She tried to hug Chloe to calm her down, but before she could do so, Chloe passed out.

12

Melanie eyed the stark white hospital walls. She sighed as she looked around the waiting area. She was waiting outside of the emergency room at Ginger Falls Community Hospital. After

Chloe passed out they'd called an ambulance. Once the ambulance had arrived the paramedics had taken Chloe to the emergency room. They'd been there for over an hour, but, they'd not allowed her to go back to see her cousin. Why was it taking so long? Looked like Chloe was just stressed and had had a panic attack.

Kyle, bless his heart, returned from the hospital cafeteria. He had two steaming cups of coffee and he'd brought her a sandwich. Her stomach felt like it was tied in a million little knots. She didn't think she could eat a sandwich right now. He pushed the tattered, dog-eared magazines aside before carefully setting the items on the small table in front of her. "You need to eat something, Mel. You haven't had anything to eat in a while."

She shook her head. "I'm too nervous to eat." She rubbed her stomach. "I feel nauseous."

"Did you call your Uncle Larry yet?"

She took a deep breath. "Not yet. I need to. I was going to wait to see what the doctor said before I call him."

He left and then returned with a can of ginger ale and a cup of ice. "Drink this. It will settle your stomach." He poured the drink into the cup and presented it to her. She sipped the liquid. It felt good and sweet on her tongue. She was surprised to discover how thirsty she was. She drank the entire soda in a few minutes. Kyle got her another. She slowly sipped the beverage.

Thankfully the doctor approached them.

She quickly stood up as Kyle stood beside her. "Is Chloe okay? Can I see her?"

The young, dark-haired doctor pushed his glasses up on his nose. "Yes, you can see her. Looks like she had a panic attack. She also has elevated blood pressure. So sad when I see cases of alleged abuse when the woman never wants me to do anything to help. Looks like she should be filing a police report." He shrugged. "But, she won't admit to being abused. She told me she accidentally fell." He glanced at her chart. "Because of her condition, we're going to admit her overnight for observation. She should be able to return home tomorrow."

Melanie leaned toward the doctor. "What condition? Are you talking about her black eye? The bruises? Elevated blood pressure?"

The doctor widened his eyes. "No, I'm talking about the baby. She's two months pregnant so we need to be careful."

Melanie didn't realize she was still holding the ginger ale until she dropped it. Icy cold liquid spilled onto the pristine white floor.

Kyle quickly grabbed some Kleenex from a nearby tissue box. He mopped up the spill. He overheard the doctor telling a staff member to send the cleaning lady up to wipe down the floor. When he rejoined Melanie, she was still speaking with the doctor. He seemed sympathetic. "I just assumed you knew she was pregnant. Chloe gave me permission to share her diagnosis and medical information with you. Perhaps she didn't realize her permission included my telling you about her pregnancy." He again consulted his chart. "She'll be in room 313. Take the elevator up to the third floor and turn left. You'll be able to visit her in an hour."

Melanie dropped into a chair. She just sat there, limp as a rag doll. Whoa. He wasn't even sure what he was supposed to say.

What could he do to help?

"I can't believe this." She mumbled the words. It was almost as if she could barely move her lips. "What am I going to do?"

"I think you need to call your uncle. He needs to know that Chloe is in the hospital and that she's expecting."

She leaned over and dropped her head in her hands. She looked defeated. "This is just too much."

He patted her back. "Calm down. Do you want me to hold your hand while you call him?"

She nodded. After she'd accessed her uncle's number on her phone, the call went through. She pressed the phone to her ear while he held her hand. "Uncle Larry. This is Melanie. Call me as soon as you get this message. It's important." She ended the call. "His voicemail picked up. I hope he'll call back soon."

She squeezed his hand. They sat together holding hands. *Jesus, we need your help right now.* He leaned back and silently prayed while they held hands for an hour. He felt his palm getting moist and she released his hand. "Kyle."

"Yes?"

"Thanks so much for bringing me here and staying with me....and...well for everything. You're a good friend."

He wasn't sure what to say. He'd hoped they could be more than friends, well, sometime in the future. If she could see past his multiple faults. "You're a good friend, too, Mel. I'm happy to help you." He pointed to the clock on the wall. "It's been an hour. You should probably go up and visit Chloe."

"Don't you want to come with me?"

"I think you should see her alone. I doubt she'd want me in the room. She doesn't know me very well...and...you saw how she reacted when I tried to talk to her in the car."

"Yes. I guess you're right. I wasn't thinking."

"When you're finished speaking with Chloe then just meet me back here. I'll stay and wait for you."

"Promise?"

He nodded. "I promise I'll be right here."

Melanie peeked into the hospital room. Chloe sat up in the bed of the semi-dark room. She had a white hospital gown on and her head was covered with a disposable blue hospital head cap. She actually smiled a little when she spotted Melanie. "Hi, Melanie." Her voice sounded a bit slurred, so, Melanie wasn't sure if she was in her right state of mind.

"Is it okay if I visit you now? Can you talk?"

She hesitated for a few seconds before she nodded. "Yes. I can talk."

Melanie had a plethora of questions to which she needed answers. But, she didn't want to overwhelm Chloe with an inquisition. The last thing she wanted to do right now would be to upset her cousin. She quietly walked into the room and sat in the chair beside the bed. She grabbed Chloe's hand and squeezed it. "Chloe, there's so many things I want to ask you, but, before I do, I just want you to know that I love you very much. I know we've not gotten along lately but, we used to be so close when you were a kid. I miss that. I was so, so worried about you when you left without saying goodbye."

"I'm sorry, Mel. Sorry I messed up."

"I've already called Uncle Larry."

Her eyes widened. "You told daddy?"

She shook her head. "I left him a voicemail a little while ago. I told him to call me back. First thing we need to do is tell your father you're in the hospital and about the baby. He'll be angry, but at least he'll know." She swallowed. "I don't know what else to say about your dad. I'm assuming your father will want me to move out of the house since he'll no longer be investing in my herb shop."

"I'm sorry Mel. I know how much that shop means to you."

That shop meant the world to her. It hurt to know that Uncle Larry would probably no longer be investing in her dream. She shrugged. "Your health is more important. Since you're pregnant you should be taking better care of yourself. You can't be around Drake anymore. At least not until he can get some help. He was hurting you and your baby. Is he the father of your child?"

Chloe didn't say anything for a long time. She finally squeezed Melanie's hand. "Yes. He's the father of my baby. When Kyle saw me crying at the beach I was on the phone with Drake. I'd told him about the baby and he was mad at first."

"Does he live near us on the Outer Banks?"

She nodded. "I met him on the beach. He didn't always have a lot of time for me because he was so busy. He told me he wants to be a singer." Again, she squeezed Melanie's hand. "That's why I took the money, Mel. He said he knew someone in Ginger Falls that could help with his singing career and that he needed money. He asked about your herb shop and your bank accounts. I told him that the herb shop belonged to me, too."

"Honey, it sounds like you were swindled. Does he have a drug problem?"

"I don't want him to get into trouble." She didn't say anything and Melanie knew not to push Chloe during this emotional time.

"Look, your dad will probably want you to return to Annapolis and live with him eventually. I honestly don't know what I'm going to do when I vacate your uncle's house. I'll probably relocate back to Annapolis and find a job there." She leaned toward her cousin. "But I want you to know that I want to be by your side while you go through your pregnancy and afterwards. I did a lousy job mentoring you, but I want to be your friend."

"You want to help me? Even if my dad doesn't help you with your shop?"

She nodded. "I care about you. I can think of some other way to help people who want to purchase herbs."

Tears slid down Chloe's cheeks. She swiped the moisture away as Melanie handed her a tissue. "Thanks so much Mel. That means a lot to me."

They silently sat, holding hands. She then recalled the engagement. She eyed Chloe's hands. No ring. "Are you and Drake engaged?"

Her mouth dropped open. "How did you know about that?"

Melanie told Chloe how her and Kyle were able to use social media to figure out that she and Drake were in Ginger Falls and had gotten engaged. She gestured toward Chloe's hand. "But I don't see a ring."

She sighed. "We're not engaged. When I found out I was pregnant I told him to marry me. We went to that jewelry store so that I could pick out a ring. He said he'd purchase the ring that I'd chosen later after his singing career took off."

She couldn't help asking the next question. "What about the money in the bank accounts? Did you and Drake spend all of it?"

She shook her head. "No. We kept it in the hotel room. Drake took care of the money. I don't know how much of it is left."

"Honey, that's your father's money." Since they'd shown up unexpectedly, it wouldn't surprise her if Drake, as well as the rest of the money, were gone. She didn't want to tell Chloe her thoughts because she didn't want to upset her. She just knew she needed to get Chloe away and back home tomorrow. She thought about Chloe's belongings in her hotel room. She also thought about Chloe's car. They'd need to drive it back to the Outer Banks. So much to think about.

"What's the matter, Melanie? You look upset."

"Nothing for you to worry about."

"No, tell me."

Well, might as well tell her the truth. "I don't want you to worry. If what I tell you upsets you then please tell me to stop and we'll worry about it later."

Chloe nodded. "Okay."

"I'm worried that Drake will take the rest of the money and leave. What if he tries to take your car?" She sighed. "Honey, we should really call the police."

"No Melanie." She actually looked frightened, so Melanie patted her hand.

"Okay. At least I wish we could go and get your car and see if your dad's cash is still in the room. Your father would want his money back."

Chloe was silent for a few minutes. She finally pointed under the bed. "There's a plastic bag under the bed. The key to my hotel room is in there."

"What?" Almost too good to be true that Chloe had the key to her room with her.

"When you and Kyle came into my hotel room, I'd already taken the room key and my car keys and was trying to leave until Drake calmed down. The keys for my car and for the room are in the pocket of my jeans." She took a deep breath. "Try not to go in there if Drake's there. He gets angry a lot and I don't want you and Kyle to get hurt." She took a deep breath. "The money is in a gray padded envelope underneath the mattress." She hugged Chloe before she rushed out of the hospital room to find Kyle.

13

Kyle sat in his SUV and eyed the door of room number three of The Snuggle Inn. No way was he going in there.

"Melanie, I know you want to get your uncle's money back but it's best if Chloe does it. It's breaking and entering if we go in there and take your uncle's money."

She held up the room key and jiggled it. "But Chloe gave us permission to go in and take the money. She told me where the money was located. She's trying to help."

"What if Drake comes back and we're in there? Honey, I think we simply need to wait until Chloe is discharged tomorrow before going in there."

"I told you not to call me Honey."

He mentally groaned. "Sorry." He enjoyed being with her so much that it was hard to remember not to call her that.

She held up the key again and pointed toward the room. "What if Drake leaves town tonight? What if he takes the money with him?"

He shrugged. "If it happens then it happens. I'm not going in there and neither are you." He looked directly at her. "You need to learn to think Mel. I was so worried when you stormed into that room earlier. What if Drake had a gun? The guy is crazy. He might have a firearm and go ballistic."

Now that made her stop and pause. Her shoulders slumped as she leaned back in the seat. "Yeah, I guess you're right. That was stupid of me." She was silent for a few minutes. "But I was worried about Chloe. I wanted to protect her."

He nodded. "Like a mom protecting her child. I get it. Really, I do. But think about it, Mel. I'm a lawyer. The last thing I need to be doing is breaking the law."

"Yes, I guess you're right." Her beautiful lips pouted. She looked so sad. They'd already determined that Drake wasn't in the room. The blinds were open and earlier they'd peeked through the window. The entire room, and the restroom, were fully visible. Not a soul in sight.

He snapped his fingers. "I have an idea. Why don't we see if we can get two rooms on this floor? We can spend the night here. Maybe we'll see Drake when he returns. At least we'll know where he is."

"What happens if we see him?"

He shrugged. "I'm not trying to get into a fight."

She rubbed her forehead. "I have a headache."

"You need to eat." He thought for a few minutes. "Let's see if we can get the rooms and then we can decide what to do from there."

A half hour later they had rooms four and

five, right beside room three. After they'd placed their luggage into their respective rooms he checked the mattresses for bed bugs in both rooms. They agreed that they needed to shower and freshen up. About an hour later Kyle met Melanie back at his car. "You'd mentioned the Christmas decorations downtown in Ginger Falls. Let's go down there and walk around and have a late dinner. When we get back you can go to bed. What time are you allowed to go and visit Chloe tomorrow?"

"Visiting hours start at nine. I was hoping Chloe would be discharged by then. But it wouldn't surprise me if she's discharged later than that."

"Okay. Once she's discharged we can come back here and she can get her stuff out of the room. Hopefully if Drake is here he won't be drugged like he was earlier."

She cringed. "This is so awful."

"Yeah, it is."

He gestured toward his car. "Come on. If you feel up to it let's go downtown. You need to get your mind off of Chloe and her problems for a little while."

They got into his car. As he made the short

trip downtown he thought about all that had gone through his mind while Melanie had been visiting with Chloe at the hospital. He'd called his brother and told him about all that had happened since they'd arrived in Ginger Falls. He'd admitted that he felt bad about being unemployed and the circumstances surrounding his unemployment. He struggled about telling Melanie that his working vacation was actually his working to find a job. Keith told him to be honest with Melanie. "I'm sure she realizes that you're a good decent person. You drove her up there to get Chloe and are giving her moral support. You could just let her know you made a mistake and that you're sorry for it. Tell her about Earl and about how important he was to you and to your sobriety." Keith had advised him.

He pulled into a parking spot right in front of a snazzy-looking restaurant. Lights twinkled from the window and a band played Christmas music on a small stage. The tables were draped with white tablecloths and a single candle glowed in the middle of each table. Perfect. Melanie had mentioned how much she enjoyed Christmas music. They could listen to some tunes while enjoying dinner. After supper they'd take a walk and look in the shop windows and admire the Christmas decorations. She'd love that. Afterwards he'd tell her all about his slip-up at work and about how he'd made a big mistake but was now rectifying the situation. Yes, that's what he'd do.

They got out of the car. "Let's eat here if you don't mind." He eyed her from head to toe. Her long brown legs were covered with blue jeans and beneath her unbuttoned coat a brown shirt tugged her trim waist. She looked so beautiful. "You shouldn't worry about calories tonight. It's Christmastime and you need to enjoy yourself." He grinned. "You look terrific, by the way."

She returned his smile. Her eyes sparkled like twin Christmas lights. "Thanks, Kyle." After they were seated she didn't even bother looking at the menu the hostess had provided. She put the menu facedown onto the table. She leaned toward him – providing him with a decent whiff of her floral perfume. He sniffed again. She smelled amazing. "Why don't you order for me?"

Wow. That was a mighty bold move for calorie-counting Melanie Richards. Looked like she was ready to have a good time so that she could forget about her problems for a little while. Their server approached with a basket of bread and butter. Kyle was more than ready to order. "I'm ordering for both of us. Filet mignon medium-well with whipped potatoes with sour cream and chives. House salad with ranch dressing." He paused. Glanced at her. "Okay if I order dessert?"

She nodded and grinned.

"Crème brûlée." He shut his menu and handed it back to the server. "Oh, and bring us a bottle of your best sparkling apple cider." He looked at Melanie and grinned. "We're celebrating."

"Of course, sir." Their server bowed before making his way back to the kitchen.

Melanie laughed. Her laughter was like sunshine on a rainy day. "Kyle why did you tell him we're celebrating?"

He playfully raised his hands in the air. "We're celebrating making this long trip in the middle of an unseasonable snowstorm. What other reason would we have to celebrate?" He smiled at her.

When their food arrived, the smell was intoxicating. His mouth watered and his stomach growled. He'd not eaten in hours.

Their server uncorked their sparkling cider and expertly poured it into their glasses. They clinked glasses before savoring a sip of the cold, sweet, snappy drink. Tasted so good. He cut into his meat. Delicious. The potatoes with sour cream and chives were excellent. The house salad and the creamy ranch dressing tasted so good.

After they'd finished their dinner their server presented them with their dessert. Melanie dipped her spoon into the crème brûlée, breaking the sugary brown layer on top. Ignoring his own dessert, he watched her while she poked her spoon into her mouth. Her eyes widened with pleasure. "Oh. My. Goodness. Ought to be a sin to have a dessert this good on planet earth."

He laughed as he enjoyed his first bite. The sugary pudding-like dessert tasted warm and decadent, almost forbidden. They ate their desserts slowly, savoring bite after bite. Since they'd already finished their cider, they washed the sweetness of their dessert away with sips of the cold water that the waiter had provided. The band started playing Silent Night. A few patrons went onto the small dance floor to slow dance to the amazing Christmas song. Feelings of warmth, gladness...and...something else rushed through him. He gently took her hand. "Dance with me, Mel?"

She grinned and squeezed his hand. "Okay."

So buoyed with happiness that it was almost as if they were floating toward the dance floor. She laid her head on his chest as he placed his arms around her trim waist. He sniffed her wonderful perfume as the notes of Silent Night, ever so softly, played from the stage. They gently slow danced. Ahh....this was heaven....or as close to heaven as he could get while on this God-given earth. They rocked and swayed to the song. When the song ended, the band stopped playing to take a break. Melanie lifted her head and looked directly at him with her hypnotic pretty brown eyes. Her full lips looked so beautiful. "Kyle..." She looked sweet, confused and speechless. He couldn't let her go. He leaned toward her and kissed her. She returned his kiss and moaned. The loud clapping from the other diners disturbed their romantic moment. She looked away for a second, as if embarrassed. Looked like they'd given the other customers a little entertainment with their impromptu kiss.

After he paid their bill he helped her put on her coat and they left the restaurant.

As they slowly walked down the street he figured it was okay to take her red-gloved hand. She stopped and looked into the window of a store that sold china figurines. Well, he needed to take Keith's advice. It was obvious that he and Melanie liked one another. He needed to come clean with her with more details about his drinking. His job situation. She might be shocked at first, but, in time, she'd learn that he'd simply made a mistake and was sorry for it. "Melanie, I needed to talk to you about something important." He said the words in a rush – before he could lose his courage.

She raised her pretty eyebrows. "Are you okay?"

He nodded. "I'm fine. I just need to talk to you about something. I wanted to wait until after dinner to tell you this."

She gestured toward a nice bench on one of the side streets. Great idea. If they sat here then they'd get some privacy. The streets were somewhat crowded with Christmas shoppers so this space was a nice reprieve. They made themselves comfortable on the bench. "Now, what did you want to tell me?" She eagerly looked at him.

"I wanted to tell you that---"

Her phone buzzed. Drat. Awful timing. She removed the phone from her coat pocket. "I have to take this call. It's Uncle Larry."

14

Melanie gripped the phone as she took her Uncle Larry's call. Her first instinct was to stand up and move away from Kyle and take the call privately – she figured Kyle wouldn't want to be further burdened with her problems. But she changed her mind. She kind of liked having him beside her while she spoke to her uncle. Kyle was already enmeshed with her problems. At this point, he probably thought she was high maintenance. "Uncle Larry. Hi."

"What is the meaning of this urgent matter? Did you find Chloe?"

She reached over on the bench and grabbed Kyle's hand. She squeezed his fingers.

"Did you not hear my question, Melanie?"

"Yes, I heard you. We found Chloe."

"We? Who is we?"

"Me and my friend Kyle. Remember you spoke to him on the phone? He rented Dale's house for his Christmas vacation. I was afraid to drive in the snow so he drove me to Ginger Falls."

"Ginger Falls? Where on earth is that? Put Chloe on the line. I want to speak to my daughter." His voice got louder and very demanding. Oh no, he was getting angry. She inwardly sighed. She needed to stand up for herself. As she squeezed Kyle's hand for strength, she realized that she didn't need such upset in her life right now. Yeah, she wanted to own her own business but not with this high of a price. Her uncle stressed her out and she didn't want to be yelled at as if she were a juvenile delinquent.

"Chloe is in the hospital."

"What?" His loud voice boomed through the phone like a cannon. "What's wrong with her? Why did you let this happen?"

Anger as thick as a boiling cauldron of soup bubbled inside of her. He'd posed the question as if *she* were responsible for Chloe's mistakes. She just couldn't deal with this anymore. "You know what, Uncle Larry? I'm so tired of this. Chloe is irresponsible. She left with a man and traveled to Ginger Falls Pennsylvania without telling me. I used social media to find her. My friend Kyle helped me to determine where she was. It took us two days to get here because of a massive snowstorm. We found her in a scary hotel room with a drug addict and she was being beaten."

"Oh my God." His voice broke. "Are you serious?"

"Yes. There's more but that's all I'm at liberty to tell you. You need to talk to Chloe. She's got a lot going on." She didn't think it was a good idea to tell him that Chloe was pregnant. She felt that news should be delivered to him by Chloe herself. She paused and took a deep breath. Her heart was pounding like a sledgehammer. She had to force herself to calm down. "Uncle, I'm so, so worried about her. I told her that I'd be beside her as her friend. I'm here to help anyway that I can. I know I didn't keep my end of the deal as far as mentoring her."

Stunning to hear nothing but silence on the line. When she heard a deep muffled noise, sounded like someone hyperventilating, the sound grew louder. That's when she realized her uncle was crying. She'd never heard her Uncle Larry cry in her entire life. He sniffed. "Will...will she die? Did he beat her badly...is she on life support?" His worried sobs carried through the phone.

"No. She was bruised and had a black eye. Elevated blood pressure. She's stressed and she needs your help."

He sniffed. "Should I call her?" So strange hearing her uncle to be out of sorts. He was always so domineering and demanding. She'd never heard him so broken and tired before. She had to assume he only acted this way in front of certain people, or when he was alone.

"I'm not sure if she has her phone with her in the hospital." She wasn't sure if she should advise him to call. What if Chloe's phone was still in the hotel room with Drake? If Chloe's dad called, would Drake have the nerve to answer the phone? She wasn't sure how that would play out. "They said they'd discharge her tomorrow. Visiting hours are at nine in the morning."

She thought of something. "I don't remember seeing a landline in the room. I think she's pretty tired. I was going to suggest that you call the hospital and ask if there's a phone in her room and they could connect you to it." She took a deep breath. "On second thought you might want to wait until the morning. I'll call you as soon as I arrive in her hospital room."

More silence. He sobbed a bit more. "Okay. We'll do what you feel is best." He sighed. "What's the name of the hospital?"

"Ginger Falls Community Hospital." When he didn't respond, she gave him the best advice she could share. "Pray for her Uncle Larry. I don't think she ever learned to deal with her mom's death. She needs help and I think connecting with you will be the first step in her healing process."

"Th...Thank you." He ended the call without saying anything else.

She slid the phone into her coat pocket. Kyle put his arm around her and she laid her head on his shoulder. He then took her hand and toyed with her fingers. He kissed each of the digits on her hand. "Are you okay?"

She sniffed his wonderful smelling cologne. Relished the feeling of his holding her. She could really get used to this. She sighed. "I'm okay. I've never heard my uncle sound like that. Never heard him cry before."

"He's shocked. I think this is a wakeup call for him."

"Yeah, I guess so."

They continued sitting on the bench. She eyed the Christmas lights on the adjoining street. Shoppers – some carrying bags and packages – ambled down the main street as they excitedly looked into the shop windows. A couple strolled by, holding hands, they stopped and shared a brief kiss before going into a store. This place sure was beautiful. She could just sit here and stare at the beautiful scenery for hours. When Kyle kissed her forehead she recalled what he'd said earlier.

She sat up straighter and looked directly into his dark brown eyes. "Before my uncle called you said you wanted to tell me something important. What was it?"

He hesitated and looked away. He dropped her hand and scratched the back of his neck. Oh no, he was hiding something. Why was he suddenly so nervous? Maybe she could calm him down. She took his hand. "Look, what's wrong? I can tell that's something's bothering you."

"I...I just don't know how you'll react when I tell you."

"Don't worry about that. Just tell me. You'll never know how I'll react until you tell me what's on your mind."

Jesus, if I ever needed your help, it's now. He needed to be careful as he told her all about his problems. Maybe he should start by focusing on what she'd revealed to him that first night in their hotel room. He focused on her lovely face. Her smooth brown skin and long dark hair, her cute smile. She looked so amazing and she'd just had an emotional phone call with her uncle. Well, she didn't look too upset. Maybe she'd already figured out that she was going to be breaking the deal with her uncle and going solo. She might want to find a job and move away from the Outer Banks.

"Do you remember that first night in the hotel room? That first place we stayed during the snowstorm?"

"Yeah? What about it?"

"You mentioned that your dad had a drinking problem and that he'd become unemployed because of it. You'd said he'd lost several jobs because of his drinking."

She nodded and touched his arm. "Is this about your sobriety? I know it's a struggle. I mean, I don't know personally, but you were open about it when we had dinner on Thanksgiving."

"Yes, this conversation is about my sobriety." He took a deep breath. "Look, when you told me that about your dad I didn't know what to say I was so shocked. You opened up and told me about your childhood, stuff that I didn't know. I was...well, I'll be honest with you. I was scared."

She tilted her head as she continued to pay attention to him. "Scared? Of what?"

He closed his eyes for a few seconds. *Tell the truth.*

The words slammed through his mind as if Jesus Christ himself were speaking directly into his ear. As he'd spent time with Melanie over the last few days, the crush he'd had on her as a child had been revitalized. "Just give me a minute. It's going to take awhile for me to tell you all of this."

"Take all the time you need."

"I had the biggest crush on you when we were kids. I've always thought that you were beautiful." She grinned and looked away as if embarrassed. "I didn't care...well...about your weight. You were always so nice and caring. I'd always wanted to get to know you better and spend more time with you." He took a deep breath. "But, you always had a crush on Keith, and, well, I just didn't think I stood a chance."

"That's so sweet. I think it's hard to tell somebody how you feel if they have feelings for somebody else." She touched his arm. "I'm glad that you told me."

"Yes. I'm glad that I finally told you, too." He paused for a few minutes. "After I got sober and started attending AA meetings I had a sponsor named Earl. He became my best friend. His drinking pattern was similar to mine – we shared similar experiences and we got along." He took a deep breath. "A few months ago Earl died of cancer."

"I'm so sorry."

He nodded toward her, acknowledging her condolences. "When I received the call that he'd died I was at a restaurant to meet a client for lunch. The client was late because of traffic. Mel, I felt so, so bad. I hadn't felt so sad since I'd gotten sober. I had a drink…then I couldn't stop. I got sloshed and when the client showed up and found me like that…well…the law firm where I worked received an angry phone call." He looked directly at her. "I got fired. I don't have a job right now. I'm looking."

Her mouth dropped open. "But…" She looked confused, turned away for a few seconds. "You haven't been working? You said you were on a working vacation."

"Well, I've been working on finding a job. I'm working with a recruiter. I was hoping to find something by the new year."

She didn't say anything for a long time. She finally looked directly at him. "I kind of sense there's more you want to say?"

"Actually yes. I just wanted to give you some time to digest the first part before I tell you the second part."

She frowned. "The second part?"

"Yeah."

She raised her eyebrows. "Actually, I have a question."

"Go ahead. Ask me anything you want. I promise to tell you the truth."

"Why are you renting Dale's house for a month if you're not working? I'd think you would've stayed home in Annapolis. Why would you spend so much money if you're not even working? I guess you could afford it?"

Whoa, he wasn't expecting her to ask him that. Well, good thing that she did. It was a great lead-in to telling her the rest of his secret. "Keith thought it would be a good idea for me to get away. He gave me my allowance so that I could rent Dale's place."

"What?" Her voice cracked through the cold night air like an angry whip. "What do you mean? Sounds like you're a child or something."

Oh no, she was getting angry. In a way, Keith had to take the lead and treat him like a child when it came to money and alcohol. How pathetic was that? Maybe he shouldn't have called it an allowance. Bad choice of words. "Look, Mel. When my dad died years ago he left Keith the entire inheritance. I was bitter and angry. I spent a lot of my evenings and weekends drinking. My fiancée broke up with me because my drinking had gotten worse because I was so bitter towards my brother. I'd burn through money like fire. I'd overspend, taking lavish trips. Buying things that I didn't need because I felt so empty. I'm so ashamed of myself. I thought my dad was showing favoritism towards my brother since my brother stayed with him, helped to care for him, until he died." He took a deep breath. "Keith...he's so kind. He was patient with me. When I got angry with him he never got angry back." He took another deep breath. "Do you realize when he told me he wanted to be a pastor that I made fun of him? That was so awful of me. I know he's forgiven me for it, but, how could I mock somebody for wanting to bring people to Jesus?"

Her anger softened. She wasn't frowning anymore, she just looked sad. Well, he needed to hurry up and tell her everything before he lost his nerve. "The bank called Keith one day stating that the payment was due for my dad's safe deposit box. We didn't know about his safe deposit box until that day. My dad had not made the payment because he'd died. My dad had listed Keith as the person who should receive the contents of the box after his death." He took a deep breath. "In the box was a letter from my dad to Keith. It told the reasons why he'd given Keith control of the inheritance and that he was supposed to pay me my share how he saw fit."

"You know my brother. Responsible. I went to him because I was broke and I wanted money. He told me about the letter. He's been giving me the inheritance in installments. He gave me my money early this year because he felt that I needed a vacation. He knew that Dale had a nice house near the beach. He knows how much I love the water. He thought I needed to get away." Might as well tell her the rest. "I also rented Dale's house because I wanted to be near you. I've always liked you. I wanted to get to know you better."

"Kyle...this is...I don't know what to say."

"Are you mad at me?"

She shook her head. "I just don't know how I feel about us spending any more time together. I'm glad you told me the truth, but, when you mention how the drinking affected your life, your finances, how you're unemployed because of your drinking - I think about my dad. One time my dad didn't have a job and all our credit cards were maxed out. We didn't have food for an entire month."

"What?" Sounded like he didn't believe her.

"No food for a month. It was awful. My mom didn't want anybody to know about it. I was enrolled at an expensive private school yet we had no food to put on the table. My mom got food from food banks. Somehow some relatives found out and they stepped in to help. The arguments got worse between my parents that month." Her lip quivered as if she were going to cry. But she pulled herself together. "Far as I know that was the first time my dad hit my mom. They separated for a few months before she went back to him. Drinking and joblessness wreaks havoc on a family." She shook her head. "I just don't know how I feel about seeing somebody who follows the same pattern as my father. Even now my dad has his moments when he doesn't act right. My mom stays with him but, I know how upsetting and stressful it can be for her."

"Mel, please don't say that. We've just started getting to know each other and—"

She shook her head. "Kyle. I just don't know if it's a good idea. I'm so, so sorry about your dad dying and about Earl dying. I can tell you were hurting. I just...I don't know. I feel kind of shocked right now."

He wasn't sure what else he could say. Maybe he could say or do something on their drive back to the Outer Banks to change her mind. He felt defeated right now. He thought about a boxing match he'd watched a few months ago. Sometimes you just get knocked down and you're too tired to get back up.

15

He couldn't sleep. Melanie had been quiet while they drove back to the hotel. He'd wanted to kiss her goodnight, but knew it was a bad idea. She looked so stunned and sad. Maybe once they spoke in the morning things would be better. He paced his hotel room. The thought of having a drink consumed him. He needed to do something to take his mind off of Melanie. He opened the door and stepped outside. The cool crisp air was like a splash of water against his heated skin. He looked up at the sky. The stars were bright as Christmas lights.

Melanie's room was right next to his. The blinds were shut. Good. This hotel was sleazy and he didn't want anybody peeking into her window. He walked a few steps and stopped in front of door number three. He peeked through the window. Blinds were still open and the room was still empty. It was almost midnight and he was worried about Drake. What if he was back in the hotel room when Chloe was discharged? Would Mel and Chloe be able to retrieve Larry's money from underneath the mattress? Well, he wanted to make sure everything was okay when they returned from the hospital. He returned to his room and paced. He opened the dresser drawer and spotted a Gideon's Bible. This was just what he needed to do. He normally read the Bible on his phone or on his laptop. For some reason, tonight he wanted to physically touch the pages while reading.

What a relief that he'd figured out what he needed to do. He pushed the small end-table to the window. The room only had one chair. He pushed the chair up to the table. He scanned the room. He needed paper. Wait, he recalled the legal notepads he kept in his trunk. He went out to his vehicle and returned with the yellow pad of paper and a pen. Starting with the New Testament, he started reading Matthew chapter 1. Focusing on the words printed on the page he read for a few hours. When words affected him, or if he had a question about something, he wrote it in his legal pad. A car door slamming interrupted him. He quickly peeked out the window. Good, it wasn't Drake.

A little tired but not wanting to go to bed, he decided to drink one of the cold coffee drinks he'd brought with him. He got some ice and poured his drink into a plastic cup. He spent the rest of the night reading the Bible, taking notes, and drinking iced coffee. Whenever he heard a noise outside he stopped reading and went to investigate. Still no Drake.

The sun was starting to rise. He stood up and yawned. Far as he could recall, he'd never read the Bible for seven hours straight.

He blinked. He wanted to be awake when it was time for Melanie to return to the hospital. He went outside to check Drake's room one last time. Still empty. It'd probably be a few hours before Melanie would be ready to return to the hospital. He returned to his room and closed his blinds. Exhaustion consumed him. He struggled to remove his shoes. He just wanted to sleep for a little while. He finally managed to get his shoes off. Still completely dressed he fell into bed - too exhausted to even put his night clothes on. He silently prayed as he fell asleep.

Kyle struggled to open his eyes. Between the crevices of the blinds, fingers of bright sunlight spilled into the room. He sat up and looked at his phone. Drat. He'd forgotten to charge it. He found his charger and plugged the phone into the wall. After he did so, he spotted a cream-colored envelope on the floor. His name was written in nice handwriting. He inwardly cringed.

This was probably a Dear John letter that

Melanie wrote and then slid underneath the door. She was probably going to tell him that she didn't want to spend time with him anymore. Clutching the letter, he returned to the bed and sat down. He took several deep breaths. *Lord, I do not have the courage to open this letter.* His charging phone buzzed.

A text from Melanie had come through a couple of hours ago.

He forced himself to read the text.

Tried to contact you this morning but couldn't. You didn't answer when I knocked on your door. Heard you snoring. Sounded like you were tired. Uncle Larry is here. Chloe was released from hospital. Doctor said she must be taken home immediately to rest. All three of us have left for Outer Banks. Don't want Uncle Larry to upset her – so must go to keep Chloe calm during the trip. We're driving Chloe's car. Read my letter. Explains everything. Luv, Mel.

Luv? Well, that was a start, wasn't it? Maybe she'd agree to their being friends at least. Friends? He liked her too much to be just a friend. If he could spend more time with her, he could imagine he'd end up falling in love with her. He finally slid his finger under the flap of the sealed envelope.

The envelope ripped as he opened it. He removed the piece of paper.

Dear Kyle,

I'm sorry if I seemed like I was cold and uncaring last night. When I'm shocked, well, it takes me awhile to gather my thoughts and speak what's on my mind. I'm grateful to you for helping me to find Chloe and for driving with me to Ginger Falls. I enjoyed being with you over the last few days and I'm glad you made the effort to reconnect with me. You were honest with me about your feelings last night. It's my turn to be honest with you. I always had a crush on your brother when we were kids but, I always thought of you as being mysterious. I'd wonder about you but never tried to find answers to my unasked questions.

Spending time with you has been a blessing. I know you'd mentioned going to Ginger Falls because of your mom? You'd mentioned you were not at liberty to talk about the information you'd discovered about her? I hope you are able to rectify all that's going on with what you were seeking in this town.

Regarding our spending time together in

the future?

I don't know.

Do you ever feel like so much is going on in your head that you need time to untangle everything? I guess that's how I'm feeling right now. I need some time to think, reflect and pray. I feel like my life is somewhat of a mess right now and I just need to figure everything out.

I'm sorry that you're driving home by yourself. I feel bad about that since you escorted me to Ginger Falls in the first place. I was wondering how you would feel about this – could we reconnect on Christmas day? You'd mentioned not having Christmas day plans and neither do I. This will give me time to think about everything, and I sense that you might have some thinking to do too? I'll still be in my uncle's house until the New Year, across the street from you. I'll explain more about that if you agree to meet up with me. It's fine if you want to meet after Christmas. Just let me know.

Luv, Melanie

Christmas day? That was three weeks away. Hard to wait that long to speak to her. He read the letter once, twice, three times. Man. What unasked questions was she referring to? He was surprised that Melanie even thought about him at all when they were kids. He didn't blame her for wanting some time to think and pray. He eyed the Bible sitting on the table. Lord willing, she'd agree that they had something wonderful between them, that could grow into something special, if she just gave him a chance. He couldn't guarantee that he'd never mess up but he'd certainly give it his best shot.

His phone buzzed.

Keith.

He accepted the call. "Kyle, you okay?"

"No."

"What's wrong?"

He eyed the letter. No, he wasn't going to tell Keith about that. Too personal. Being around Melanie was so addictive, but, addictive in a good way. He missed her already. But, she did have a point. She'd brought up the other reason he'd traveled to Ginger Falls. He wanted to know more about his mom. He'd hoped that looking up his grandmother might be a way to know more about his mom. Being around Melanie felt euphoric, so euphoric that he'd not thought much about Phoebe White since he'd been in town.

Maybe it was best that Melanie had left Ginger Falls. He still had something he wanted to do and it was best he do this alone. "Kyle?"

Oh, he needed to let his brother know what he was planning on doing. "I'm going to our grandmother's house."

"Kyle." His brother's shocked voice jumped from the phone like a speeding bullet. "We said we'd meet up with her together if she agreed."

"I know. I didn't say I was going to meet her. I'm going to her house to see if...well...maybe I can catch a glimpse of her."

"So, you're just going to drive over to her house and sit there? That's it?"

Yeah, it sounded kind of weird but it was what he felt like doing. "I figure since I'm here I might as well." He quickly told Keith all that had occurred in Ginger Falls, omitting the letter and his dinner date with Melanie.

"That's rough. So, you don't know how Chloe's doing now?"

"No." Actually that wasn't a bad idea. He

was so enmeshed thinking about Melanie and his feelings for her, that he'd not asked about Chloe. He wanted and needed to know if she was alright. He then remembered Drake. Hopefully he'd not returned before Chloe had gone to get her things from the room. "Hold on."

He quickly texted Melanie.

Thx for the letter. Chloe okay? He figured she must be if they allowed her to go home from the hospital.

Chloe's fine. She must take it easy for the rest of the pregnancy.

He replied.

Good to hear she's okay. Drake? Stayed up all night reading Bible and stayed on lookout for Drake. He didn't return to hotel last night. Did Chloe get money back from Drake?

A few seconds later Melanie texted back.

Thanks for looking out for Drake. He's gone. Not sure where he is. Chloe got Dad's money.

He itched to hang up on Keith and call Melanie. But she said she needed time so he was not going to bother her. Well, he'd leave her alone. But he needed to respond to her invite.

Glad you got money back. Not sure what to say about Drake. Be careful.

See you on Christmas. Luv, Kyle.

A few minutes later she responded.

Okay. See you on Christmas.

"Kyle?" Oh, he had to talk to Keith.

"Look, I'll call you back in a little bit. I'm not breaking our promise. I won't attempt to meet her or anything like that."

"Are you sure you're okay? You sound funny."

"It was a rough night." What time was it anyway? He eyed his phone and saw that it was one in the afternoon. He figured it was late in the day. "Bye." He hung up before Keith could question him further. He silently prayed while he brushed his teeth and washed up. After he'd gotten dressed he stepped outside. He quickly peeked through the window of Drake and Chloe's room. He heard adult voices. Luggage stacked on the beds and a kid was running around the room. He quickly looked away, not wanting to be caught looking into the room of strangers. Since Chloe checked out looked like Drake wouldn't be able to return to this room. Hopefully Drake would leave Chloe alone. He'd not want her to get upset and get sick as she'd done last night.

The scent of fried meat and bread wafted around him. His stomach rumbled. Man, he was starving. His mouth watered. The smell was coming from a nearby pancake house. He got into his car and closed his eyes. No, he wasn't going to eat anything. He was going to fast for the day. He had some bottled water in the back seat. He opened one of the bottles and drank. The water was ice cold and so good going down his parched throat. He drank so quickly that some of the water ran out of the side of his mouth and dribbled down his chin. He wiped the stray water away with the back of his hand. He drank the entire bottle before opening another and sitting it in the cup holder between the two front seats.

He typed the address into his GPS. 2700 Cornflower Lane Ginger Falls Pennsylvania. *Lord, please be with me. Amen.*

16

Kyle sat in his car across the street from the house with a white picket fence. The numbers 2700 were boldly emblazoned on the mailbox. The house was in a nice residential community. He'd seen a few people out taking a midday stroll. Some were walking their pets. He'd seen some families outside stringing Christmas lights to their homes. A few residents had given him curious stares. He supposed he looked strange sitting on the street doing nothing. He'd moved his car a few times so that he didn't look so obvious sitting in the same spot. He'd been sitting on the street for two hours staring at Phoebe White's house.

Two little boys exited a nearby home and started a snowball fight. They laughed as they shot the balls through the air like tiny cannons. Just seeing the fight reminded him of the snowball fight he'd had with Mel. He didn't know how he'd manage not to see her again until Christmas. Could he wait that long? He closed his eyes as he reminisced about their kiss in the snow. So totally amazing.

The sound of an approaching car broke his reverie. His eyes shot open and he honed in on the vehicle. A taxi. An old White woman exited the car. She wore a long winter coat and had a hat on her head. Her arms were full of colorful shopping bags of what he assumed were Christmas presents. She slowly walked toward number 2700. That couldn't be Phoebe White. Maybe it was a roommate or maybe Phoebe rented the house to this old lady.

The two boys ceased their snowball fight as they rushed toward the woman. They hugged her. Her loud cheerful laughter reminded him of sleigh bells on this cold sunny day. "Ms. Phoebe!" Both boys yelled the woman's name with joy.

His heart thundered like a sledgehammer as he openly stared at the threesome.

One of the boys looked directly at the old woman. "Did you bake cookies this morning?"

"Yes. Gingersnaps. Go ask your mom if you can have some cookies and milk. Afterwards you can help me bring up my Christmas decorations from the basement."

The two boys rushed back toward their home. The slam of their front door resounded on the otherwise quiet street. Ms. Phoebe glanced across the street at the boys' home before she spotted him sitting in his car.

She looked directly at him.

What was he supposed to do? He couldn't just go up to her and say that he was her grandson. Hearing that might cause this old lady to have a heart attack. Besides, he'd promised Keith he wouldn't do anything. Shock coursed through him. It was almost as if he were as frozen as the snowman in the nearby yard. She nodded toward him, as if saying hello. He waved back before quickly driving away.

He pulled into the parking lot of a nearby Seven Eleven and took several deep breaths. He vacantly stared at customers breezing in and out of the store carrying containers of milk and plastic bags of groceries. He sat there for an hour. It took him that long to calm down and figure out what to do. Never in a million years would he ever have thought that his grandmother was White. He stared at his hands before rubbing his arm. He looked at his brown skin. He'd always assumed both of his mother's parents were African-American. In the few pictures he'd seen of his mom she had medium brown skin.

So stunning. Amazing to find out something about himself that he didn't know. Wow. Also amazing to be physically close to somebody who was biologically connected to his mother. He needed to talk to somebody. His phone buzzed.

Keith.

He accepted the call. "Kyle. You said you'd call me later."

He didn't respond.

"What's wrong?"

"I think I'm in shock."

"Huh? Are you sick?"

Was he sick? Not really. He wondered if Phoebe had any other kids. Did he and Keith have White relatives? Did Phoebe give their mom up for adoption because the father of her baby was Black? Was their grandfather alive too? Who was he?

"Kyle? Man, what's wrong? Did something happen when you went to Phoebe White's house?"

He finally managed to respond. "Yes."

"What happened?"

"Keith. She's White."

"Yes, her name is Phoebe White."

"*No.* I mean she's White. Caucasian."

Shocked silence. "Are you serious?"

"Yes."

"Wow. That's surprising."

"Yes. It is. I'm going back to the hotel to lie down. I'll call you when I get there."

Melanie pushed the vacuum cleaner across the carpeted floor. She'd already scrubbed the windows, cleaned the bathroom, and mopped the kitchen. Once she was done vacuuming she wrapped the cord around the vacuum cleaner and put it into the hall closet. She dropped into a chair. Exhaustion swept through her but, she didn't want to stop moving. Cleaning always helped her whenever something was on her mind. Even though she was tired she put her coat on and took a walk on the beach.

The sun sparkled against the frigid waves. She could still see some remnants of snow clinging to the sides of houses. It'd been over a week since she'd seen Kyle and she missed him like crazy. She didn't want to wait until Christmas to see him but, she figured she'd made the right decision. She still had so much to think about. If her and Kyle were to see one another regularly what would happen? The chemistry between them sizzled like grease hitting a hot skillet. What would happen if he had another disappointment? Would he turn to alcohol? What if he wasn't safe after a drinking binge? What if he drove drunk?

What did he find out about his mom recently? She knew that it was a personal subject for him but she still wondered about it. Oh, the thoughts about Kyle tumbled in her head like scattering snowflakes. The wind blew across her face. She stopped walking and simply stared at the beach. *Lord, please be with Chloe. I'm still worried about my cousin. Amen.* After they'd arrived back from Ginger Falls Uncle Larry had taken charge. He'd apologized to her about Chloe's erratic behavior. They'd had a heart-to-heart talk and he'd agreed that Chloe needed to come and live with him in Annapolis.

Uncle Larry had said that he wanted to keep an eye on Chloe and he was fearful about Drake. He sounded dangerous and he didn't want him to return to Outer Banks to reunite with Chloe. He'd urged Melanie to come live with them for the time being – just in case Drake decided to return and try to harm her.

She doubted Drake would come to her herb shop and she wasn't worried. She pointed out to her uncle that if Drake wanted to reunite with Chloe there was nothing to stop Chloe from leaving again. He'd been angry when she told him that. He felt that Chloe had been affected by being in the hospital – she now better realized the gravity of her situation and knew she needed to be safe, especially when it came to the baby. She didn't argue with him. Hopefully he was right.

Her Uncle Larry had mentioned that her mentoring Chloe had not worked out. She told him that she would be seeking employment and moving back to Annapolis once she found a job and an apartment. He kindly allowed her to stay in the house on Outer Banks until she'd made all of her arrangements. She told him that she would like to stay until the new year at least and he'd been okay with that. He had said she could take as long as she needed to relocate – it was the least he could do considering all she'd had to go through to attempt to mentor Chloe.

It was so cold outside her face had grown numb. She returned to her house and made a cup of sugar-free hot chocolate. A text came through her phone. She glanced down at the screen. Juli, the pastor's wife. Melanie had not been to church in a couple of weeks. Juli had probably noticed. She had a rapport with Juli and sometimes they went out to Starbucks for coffee after church.

Instead of responding to the text she called.

"Hi, Juli."

"Melanie. Where have you been? The last time we had coffee you said that you were having problems with Chloe. I would have contacted you sooner but I didn't want to be too nosy. I figured you'd let me know if you wanted to talk about it some more." Juli had told her once that some parishioners would get offended when she asked why they'd disappeared or had not been to church. She knew that the pastor's wife was genuinely concerned and wanted to help.

"I'm sorry. I've been meaning to call you. So much has happened over the last couple of weeks." She sighed. "Actually, I need a friend right now. I'd talk to you about everything that's been going on but I'm just so tired. I was going to go take a nap."

"Oh, Melanie. You sound a bit upset. Just grant me another minute of time. I wanted to ask you something."

"Sure."

"Tomorrow the church is serving Christmas lunch to the homeless. We're short on volunteers. Will you come to the soup kitchen and help us prepare the food and serve it?"

"I'd be glad to."

"Wonderful. Afterwards we can have a nice long chat."

"Okay." That sounded like just what she needed.

"Could you bring some of those disposable chafing dishes for the food? I think you'd mentioned you had some at your house."

"Sure, no problem." She'd found the chafing dishes in the basement of the house. She'd asked her Uncle Larry if she could donate them to her church and he'd agreed. After she ended the call she trudged up the stairs. She laid down on the bed. She really needed a nice long nap.

17

Kyle pushed himself hard as he could as he ran along the beach. The sun touched the horizon with a golden glow. In spite of the cool temperatures sweat rolled down his face. His mind cluttered with the information that he'd recently found out about his mom's mother.

So weird calling Phoebe White his grandmother. He'd kept his promise to Keith. He'd not read his mom's journal nor had he gone through the rest of her things. They would do that together soon, Lord willing. He kept thinking about Phoebe White hugging those children and telling them she'd made gingersnaps. Did she like to bake? Keith had always loved cooking and baking. Since his sobriety he himself had discovered how much he loved cooking. Perhaps both of them had inherited their love for cooking from Phoebe. Was it possible to inherit cooking talent?

He rounded a corner and stopped running. Whew. What a workout. As he slowly walked through town for his cool down he thought about his job situation. He'd been busy working with his recruiter and had had some phone interviews for jobs. The recruiter had mentioned that if a second interview was requested then he'd probably have to travel to Annapolis to do the interview in person. Well, if he had to go back during his vacation then so be it. Hopefully he'd find a job before Christmas. Reason being, if he had a job, that would improve his chances with Melanie. At least he thought it would improve them.

He glanced across the street as he approached his temporary home. Melanie came out of her house.

She looked amazing.

She wore red pants and a Christmas sweater. She had a red Santa hat perched on her head. Her arms were full of chafing dishes. Hmm. Where in the world was she going dressed like that? The urge to rush forward and open her car door for her – help her to put those big dishes into her back seat – tumbled through him. He squelched the urge. He'd agreed that he'd keep his distance until Christmas, so he had to honor that.

Hey, but helping her out right now...well...was that off limits? What if she really needed his help? She looked over at him and caught him blatantly staring. How embarrassing. He was looking at her like a love-sick fool. He had to wonder if she'd even thought about him since they went their separate ways in Ginger Falls. He might as well say something. "Good morning, Mel. Need some help?"

She shook her head. "No thanks. I'm good." She quickly opened the back seat of her car and put the dishes into her vehicle. Good grief. This was ridiculous. He'd already made a fool of himself staring at her. He had to make himself go into his house. If he didn't, he'd make an even bigger fool of himself by staring at her driving away.

He guzzled a bottle of water before dropping into a chair in the living room. He eyed his mother's boxes before staring at her journal that he'd put aside. *When* were he and Keith going to go through all of this stuff? Keith was busy pastoring his church. His wife Karen had mentioned how busy things were since they'd had the twins. The twins were almost one. Karen had said that one of them was starting to walk. His phone buzzed.

Keith. They'd had numerous conversations about their grandmother since they'd discovered her in Ginger Falls. Whenever they'd wonder about something, they'd call or text one another to voice their thoughts. He heard an approaching car as he accepted the call. "Keith. What's up?"

"I know you're anxious to go through our mom's stuff."

"Yeah?"

"Well, now's the time." Excitement filled his voice. Kyle frowned. What in the world was he talking about?

"What do you mean? You're not here."

"Yes, we are."

"We?"

"Open your front door."

He opened the door and spotted Keith's SUV parked in the driveway behind his. A Christmas tree was tied to the roof of the vehicle. He rushed over to the car just as Keith exited. Gladness, as fresh and cool as spring rain, buoyed up within him. He hugged his brother hard. Normally he wasn't so affectionate but, he just couldn't help himself. He wanted...no he needed to see his twin. Shame filled his soul as tears rushed from his eyes. He quickly turned away, not wanting them to see him cry.

"Hey man, you alright?" Keith clapped him on the shoulder. He quickly nodded as he pulled himself together. He glanced into the backseat. Karen was taking one of the twins from the car seat. Maybe he should help her. Would the kid start crying if he tried to remove him from the seat? Keith must've known what he was thinking because he expertly removed his other son from the car seat. "You can carry Peter inside. He's not walking yet but Mark is walking a little bit."

Whoa. This kid was heavy. Kids grew so fast. It'd been a few months since he'd seen the twins. Unable to resist he kissed the boy's chubby brown cheek. Karen approached carrying the other baby. "Peter is friendly. It will probably take Mark awhile to warm up to you since he hasn't seen you in a long time."

As soon as all of them were inside Karen and Keith worked together quickly setting up the playpen. She set Mark into the playpen and scanned the house. "Kyle, I'm going to have to put covers over your electrical sockets."

"Okay."

She did a few things which she called babyproofing the house. After the kids were fed both of them fell asleep. She put them into the playpen for their nap. While the twins napped Keith brought in the Christmas tree. They'd brought tinsel, decorations, lights, everything they needed. A couple of hours later the brightly lit tree was in front of the large bay window. Looked amazing. Keith had brought some extra

Christmas lights and those they'd strung outdoors down the railing and lights were also placed on the large bush in his yard. He wondered if the twins would get excited when they spotted the Christmas tree and lights.

Keith went to the store to get groceries. Karen sat in the kitchen with Kyle. They'd already eaten their lunch and were enjoying cups of coffee. Karen blew air through her lips. "What a night."

Kyle chuckled. "So, all of you are staying here through Christmas?"

She looked at him and smiled. "Until New Year's if you'll have us." She leaned toward him. "You might want to send us back after you spend a few hours with the twins."

He laughed at that. Christmas was two weeks away. If they stayed as long as she'd implied that was three weeks.

"You laugh but I'm serious. You might be ready to kick us out of the house in a few days."

He glanced at the sleeping babies in the living room. "They're nice-looking kids."

She grinned as she sipped her coffee. "Thanks."

He took his phone into the living room and

took a few pictures of the babies while they were sleeping. It'd be nice to get to know the twins. Since they'd been born he'd seen them occasionally. He wanted to be sure he became an important part of their lives.

He returned to the kitchen and took his seat. "So, you and Keith just decided to drive here overnight?"

"We've been discussing this since you found out your mother was adopted. Keith wanted to spend some time with you. He hasn't had a vacation in a long time. The assistant pastor agreed to lead the church until we return in January." She took a deep breath. "Keith has been worried about you Kyle."

Not surprising. "I've been fine." Although they'd agreed to keep the information about their mom's adoption to themselves for a while, Keith sheepishly admitted that he'd told Karen everything. Kyle was fine with that. He couldn't imagine keeping something like that from your spouse.

She touched his arm. "You've been going through a lot."

He nodded towards her. "I suppose so."

She gestured toward the window which

had a good view of Melanie's house. "Keith mentioned you'd reconnected with Melanie. I was going to go over and invite her for dinner tonight. I think she'd enjoy seeing Mark and Peter."

Oh, no. Bad idea. Since he'd not told Keith everything that'd happened between him and Melanie, he figured it was time to come clean. They needed to know about Melanie's proposed hiatus, if you could call it that.

"What's the matter, Kyle?"

"Well..." over the next hour he told Karen everything. Not knowing how many details Keith had provided he started by telling her about his Thanksgiving with Melanie. He talked for a good long while, Karen interjecting, asking questions occasionally. He told of all of the events that had occurred while they were on the road, Melanie's letter, and her proposed hiatus until Christmas. He then told her about how flustered he'd been when he'd spotted Melanie earlier that morning. "So, you see why asking her to dinner is not a good idea." He gestured toward the children sleeping in the living room. "You might want to take the kids over to visit her. I don't think she'd want to come over here."

"Melanie's been through a lot. I know she was in an abusive relationship a few years back."

"Yeah, Keith mentioned that to me, but did not tell me much."

She shrugged. "Maybe you can ask her about it. Kyle I think she likes you, but she's just scared. She's thinking about all the problems she had growing up with her dad. She's seeking stability."

Yeah, he knew that. He just didn't know what more he could do except find a job and be sure he stayed sober. He'd prayed. He'd fasted. What more could he do? "I don't know what I'm going to do if she tells me she doesn't want to spend time with me anymore."

Karen looked thoughtful as she finished her coffee and topped off their cups. After she took her seat she focused on him. "If she says she doesn't want to see you anymore then maybe you can make a suggestion."

"A suggestion?"

She nodded. "Ask if you can take things slow. Maybe see her once a week for an hour. Do that for a few months or so to prove your stability to her."

He wasn't sure if she'd agree to that if she'd already made up her mind. But, he could always try. He wasn't one to give up easily.

"Kyle, I wanted to share something with you. Did Keith tell you about my past? All that I went through before we got married?"

He frowned. He'd been bitter towards Keith for a few years. He was drinking every night, angry because their father had left Keith in charge of the inheritance. "No. As you know we were estranged for a while."

"Well, I was leery about your brother. I wasn't ready to date anybody. I was engaged."

"You were engaged when you met Keith?" This was news.

"Yes. I was engaged before I met him. My then fiancé stole money from the church. It'd been going on for a long time. He didn't do it alone. He had the help of the church secretary. Not only were the two of them stealing, they were also having an affair."

Whoa. He'd never known any of this. "Karen I'm sorry. What happened to him?"

"He and the secretary ran away together. The theft was exposed when they'd gone missing. They were eventually captured and he's doing time in prison now." Surprising that Keith had never thought to mention this to him before. "When I met your brother I was leery about men and leery about church. Some of the church members mistakenly thought that *I* was involved with the crime."

"Why would they think that?" Karen was one of the nicest women he'd ever met.

"You know how church folks can be."

Yeah, he did know. "Sounds stressful."

"It was. So, I left. I guess you could say I ran away. I didn't want to be around them anymore so I moved back home to Annapolis to live with my mom. As you know Keith was her next-door neighbor." Yeah, he remembered that. He'd met Karen's mom a few times. "Anyway, when your brother wanted to spend time with me he asked if he could see me for breakfast each morning. He took things slow." She grinned. "Plus he won me over with his tasty breakfasts. I must've gained ten pounds."

"Do you think that's what I need to do with Melanie?"

"It's worth a shot. You'll never know if it'll work until you try." Both of them were quiet as they enjoyed their coffee. He thought about what she'd just told him. Maybe there was something that he could give to Melanie on Christmas day. His gift might open the door to her agreement to spend time with him. "You look like you're thinking about something really hard."

"I am. Thanks for the advice." He quickly gave his sister-in-law a one-armed hug.

18

Melanie tossed the freshly chopped onions and garlic into the frying pan. She added the ground beef. The scent of the food made her mouth water. She'd slept late that morning and had struggled to arrive on time to assist Juli with the Christmas luncheon for the homeless. The volunteers worked together and about an hour later big chafing dishes of chili – one regular and one meatless, were set on the serving table. Juli lit the Sterno jars to keep the chafing dishes hot. Warm cornbread slathered with butter was also set out. A fresh garden salad and cookies donated by a local bakery rounded out the simple meal.

Melanie smiled as she dished out the chili for their guests. Serving others always helped to take her mind off of her problems. After all of the guests were served they were given a Christmas bag of gifts – an apple, an orange, granola bars and toiletries had been placed into each gift bag. After the guests had taken their exit, all of the volunteers stayed behind. They dished up leftover chili. They'd enjoy their meal before they cleaned up. Juli and Melanie sat together at a table in the corner. Melanie dipped her spoon into the bowl of chili. The warm tomatoes, spices and meat tasted so delicious. She bit into the warm cornbread. The buttery richness of the bread paired well with the chili. She enjoyed two large bowls, relishing the wonderful food. Juli chuckled as she finished her meal.

Melanie eyed Juli. "What's so funny?"

"You seem different. You know, since you've been volunteering here, that's the first time I've ever seen you go back for seconds. You're always worried about calories."

Calories. She'd been thinking so much about Kyle, wondering what she should do, that she'd not focused as much on how many calories were in each meal. She thought about the romantic dinner they'd shared. He'd chosen a wonderful meal for her and then he'd kissed her on the dance floor.

"What are you thinking about, Melanie?"

That's right. She needed to talk to Juli about Kyle. Tell her everything. So she told her everything that had happened between her and Kyle – starting from Thanksgiving and ending with the fact that she'd run into him earlier that morning. She gave her all the details, she even told her about the amazing kiss. Juli nodded and asked questions. She gave her undivided attention. She took a deep breath. "I just don't know what to do, Juli. I've been praying about it, thinking about it. I even talked to my girlfriends about it. Just can't seem to figure it all out."

Juli was quiet for a few minutes. She seemed to be choosing her words carefully, making sure she properly expressed herself. "Well, you and Kyle have reconnected after such a long time. You were only with him for a few days. I know it may seem longer given all that happened, but, that's not enough time to know a person." She leaned back into her chair and was silent for a minute. "From what I'm hearing he's honest. He told you what happened with his AA sponsor and about losing his job. I think he's sorry about it. We all make mistakes. None of us are perfect. You shouldn't blame Kyle because of your dad's mistakes. From what I'm hearing, he *used* to have an uncontrollable drinking problem. He'll always be an alcoholic but at least he's now getting the help he needs. Plus, he's saved now. Salvation doesn't necessarily rectify a problem, but it makes life so much easier if both you and Kyle share the same beliefs, the same faith."

"So, you think I should date him?"

"I can't advise you to date him. Do what you feel is best in your heart. It sounds like you like him. If I liked somebody and he shared my beliefs and he was honest with me about his faults then I'd consider at least giving him a chance. But that's me. I can't advise what's best for you. I'm just giving you some things to consider." She sat up straighter in her chair. "And remember the scripture in Matthew where Peter asks Jesus how often should he forgive a brother who sins against him? He asks if it should be seven times? And Jesus responds--"

"Seventy times seven." Both women said the three words at the same time.

"It's just so hard. I've been leery about men since Duane."

"Have you told him all that happened with your ex-fiancé?"

She sighed. "No. I don't really like talking about that." She'd told Juli about Duane once during one of their after-church coffee visits.

"Well, I think you might want to consider telling him about that sometime. He might want to know some of what you've been through."

She considered Juli's advice while they cleaned up the dishes and wiped down the tables and mopped the floor. Later as she drove home, she thought about the seventy-times seven Bible verse. She also thought about Kyle. He was upset about what had happened when he fell off the wagon. It weighed him down. She could tell. She then thought about her dad and the mountain of unpaid bills they'd had to contend with because he'd lost another job from his drinking. Her dad had leaned on Jesus, at least he professed to doing so. But, her dad never seemed very remorseful about his actions. From what she could tell Kyle wanted to try and do all that he could within his power not to mess up again.

It was just starting to get dark outside. She glanced at the clock on her dashboard. Four thirty. She took a quick glance across the street at Kyle's house. What in the world? She pulled into her driveway. She got out of her car and stared at Kyle's home. Christmas lights twinkled on the house and there was a fully decorated tree in the large bay window. That didn't look like something Kyle would do, go out and get a tree and decorate it? What was up with all the Christmas lights outside? Did he really do all of this? When they were on their road trip Kyle had mentioned that he never decorated for Christmas. She then noticed the second SUV in the driveway. That looked like Keith's and Karen's vehicle. She wanted to peek into the car to see if there were children's car seats in the back. That would give her a clue as to if Keith and Karen might be visiting.

No, she didn't want to do that – peek into their car. What if Kyle caught her snooping around in his driveway? If Keith and Karen were there then maybe she should stop by for a visit. No, that wouldn't do. She'd told Kyle they could meet up on Christmas day. She'd stick to what she'd proposed. Kyle had mentioned that she'd always had a crush on his brother when they were kids. Well, the fact that he'd mentioned that – made her wonder if her childhood crush still bothered him. Would he be upset if she invited Keith and his family over for dinner and didn't include him?

She mentally pushed all of those thoughts out of her mind as she went into her house. She figured Kyle may have confided to Keith or Karen about their Christmas meet up. Knowing how tenuous the situation was perhaps Keith and Karen would bring the children over to visit when they had some free time. Hopefully they would reach out to her during their visit.

"Why do you keep peeking out the window? Looking for Melanie?" Keith grinned. "Are you in love?" He said the word *love* with a long, exaggerated tone.

Kyle chuckled. "Man, be quiet." It felt good to just sit in the living room and talk and kid around with his brother for a while. Karen had just taken the twins over to Melanie's house for a visit. She said she'd try and stay for at least an hour or so. This gave them some time alone to start looking through their mom's stuff. He'd found that when the twins were awake they could be very demanding at times. Now he understood why Karen jokingly said that he might want to send them away before New Year's. He was thankful that he had a spare bedroom and an extra bathroom to accommodate his impromptu guests. He eyed the journal sitting on the shelf. "Why don't we start with the journal?"

"Sure." Both of them plopped onto the couch and Kyle opened the journal.

Thankfully their mom's beautifully scripted handwriting was easy to read. They held the journal between them and silently read for an hour. "This is boring." The journal began shortly after she'd gotten married. So far all she'd written about was what she'd cooked for meals and about how she wanted to find a job. Their dad said he wanted her to stay home. They seemed to have a lot of arguments about her working.

"Well, we have to keep reading Keith. We can probably knock through this today. If for some reason we have to put this aside for a bit when Karen comes home with the twins – we can pick it up tonight."

She dated her entries. She wasn't consistent with keeping her journal. At times she'd go for months without writing anything. *I'm pregnant.* The words screamed from the page. Things got somewhat interesting as she talked about her pregnancy. They chuckled when she mentioned how their constant movement in her womb would keep her up at night. She mentioned her cravings for ice cream, cheddar cheese and chocolate milk.

Having two babies seemed to be a lot

because after talking about her pregnancy for several entries, she didn't do a journal entry until they were six months old. She mentioned their fights and their demands. She complained about their not always playing together nicely. Kyle figured she no longer thought about getting a job since she had both of them to care for. She complained about their dad not wanting to help change their diapers. Her next entry was when they were almost three. *Had a snowstorm today. Took Keith and Kyle out to play in the snow. Sang The Snowman song to them. Kyle really liked it!*

Kyle jumped up from the couch. "Keith, I remember that."

"What?"

"I remember her singing that song while we were playing in the snow." He pointed to the top of the page. "See the date. We were almost three."

The diary turned grim. *I haven't been feeling well lately. We had to hire somebody to help me with the twins. I have zero energy.* She further spoke of her symptoms. Found out she was sick.

The door opened and Karen and the twins came into the house. Karen had the babies strapped into the double stroller. One of the kids screamed.

"Cut that screaming out. What's wrong, buddy?" Keith's loud voice boomed through the house. The screaming immediately stopped as Keith stomped over to Karen and helped her to remove the twins from the stroller. Karen spoke quietly to Keith. Something about one of the boys being upset because he didn't want to leave Melanie's house. Seeing they were busy Kyle put the journal away. He was hoping Keith wouldn't be too tired to continue reading after the twins were asleep.

Kyle made spaghetti for dinner. Since the kids ate the same food as the adults he didn't add his usual hot sauce or red pepper to the spaghetti sauce. They had some kind of portable contraption that was strapped to the kitchen chairs. This allowed the children to sit at the table while they ate. Looked like they used this because they didn't have highchairs at his house. Karen quickly cut the spaghetti up for the kids while Keith filled their sippy cups with some kind of drink. One of the twins, he believed it was Peter, looked at him and smiled. Peter waved. "Hi." Kyle hadn't really heard them say many understandable words, so he was surprised.

Kyle grinned. "Hi, Peter." Hopefully he had the name right. He needed to spend more time with the kids so that he could learn to tell them apart. He remembered how he used to get annoyed when folks would confuse him with his brother.

Karen glanced up from her chore. "You can tell them apart?"

He might as well be honest. "No. I just assumed it was Peter because earlier you'd told me that he's more friendly." He had wanted to ask Keith and Karen if they needed help fixing the kids' plates – but they seemed to have an easy rhythm going and he didn't want to disrupt their flow. After dinner there was clean up, baths, diaper changes, pajamas...just watching the two of them made him tired...he'd not thought much about having kids but, man, what a lot of work.

Kyle read them a bedtime story and the kids were asleep by eight. Karen stayed in the bedroom with the twins while Keith and Kyle continued reading their mom's journal. The rest of the journal focused on her illness and the fact that she'd hired a private investigator. There were minimal entries. *I don't have much time left. I don't want to die and leave my babies without a mother. I love them so much. I don't want to leave my husband – he'll be without a wife when I die and that makes me sad. In spite of all our arguments he's the most important man to me on this earth. We've been arguing about Phoebe White. He doesn't want me to meet up with her. I want to contact her but don't know if I'm strong enough to face a disappointment now. What if she rejects me? After much prayer and reflection, I've decided not to contact Phoebe. I will leave the entire matter in the Lord's hands before I go to meet my Maker.* This last journal entry gave them the answer to one of the questions they'd been wondering about.

Both of them stared at the page, silent. "I guess she didn't meet her." Keith spoke first.

"Does that mean we're supposed to meet up with her? Should we contact her?"

"I'm not sure if we should."

Kyle closed his eyes and again relived the moment when he'd seen Phoebe with those children. The gingersnap cookies. Christmas presents. Snowball fight. From first appearances, it seemed like those kids adored Phoebe. If she adored those kids then she'd not shun her own child, or in this case her own grandchildren. He thought about Mark and Peter. They were related to Phoebe. What if she wanted to meet them, too?

"Keith, I think we should send her a couriered letter. We should write it tonight."

"Kyle..." Keith looked worried. He didn't want to do it unless his brother agreed.

"I want to do this Keith."

Keith clapped him on the shoulder. "Man, I'm worried about what will happen if she doesn't want to meet us."

"But we'll never know unless we contact her."

"If she doesn't want to meet us...I'm well, I'm concerned about how that will affect you."

What Keith was implying slammed into him like a ton of bricks. "You're afraid that I'm going to start drinking again if Phoebe rejects us." The anger in his voice boomed from his mouth like a cannon. In the bedroom, one of the twins started crying. Drat, he'd woken up one of the kids. Karen closed the bedroom door. They heard her cooing to the child, trying to get him to fall back to sleep. Thankfully she didn't come out to reprimand them for being too noisy. He needed to cool down. "I'm going for a walk."

"Hey, Kyle don't be mad."

He shook his head. He didn't want Keith to get the wrong idea. "I'm not. I just need to get some air." He shoved his arms into his coat and put a hat on his head. "Tell Karen I'm sorry that I woke up one of the kids."

19

Kyle walked in the frigid cold night on the boardwalk. Christmas lights twinkled from the lampposts and store windows. Most of the shops were closed. He passed a bar and a few restaurants that were still open. If Phoebe rejected them he'd be okay. He'd be disappointed, but, he felt he was strong enough not to go on a drinking binge. He'd try his best, with the Lord's help, not to make the same mistake he'd made when Earl had died. He just needed to convince Keith that he could handle Phoebe's possible rejection. He walked for over an hour.

He returned to his house. Good. The living room light was still on. Keith was probably still awake. The lights on the Christmas tree winked in the dark night. He opened the door and spotted Keith waiting for him in the living room. Before Kyle could open his mouth Keith stood up, clearing his throat. "Look Kyle. I was praying the entire time you were out for your walk. We can write the letter tonight and send it courier tomorrow. I just need you to promise me to reach out if you're feeling bad if she decides not to meet us. I don't want you to—"

"I know what you're going to say. I promise I'll let you know if I feel bad." He mentally sighed with relief. Good, Keith had agreed. They stayed up all night drafting the letter. They finally finished the final draft right before the twins woke up. Karen was going into the kitchen with the kids to get their breakfast while Kyle printed the letter. He went into his office to remove the paper from the printer. He scanned the letter one last time.

Dear Phoebe White,

In 1966 you gave birth to a female child which you gave up for adoption. Her adoptive parents named her Louvenia Greene. Her married name was Louvenia Baxter. We are Louvenia's identical twin sons, Keith and Kyle Baxter. We wanted to know if you would be willing to meet us. We're curious to meet you since you are our biological grandparent. We will understand, and respect, if you are unwilling to meet. We are happy to converse with you via phone, email or snail mail, if you wish, prior to our proposed meeting. Our contact information is below. We are residing at the Outer Banks address until New Year's Day.

Both of them signed the letter. Kyle slid the letter into a padded envelope. As an afterthought they also placed their business cards into the envelope. Kyle grabbed his coat. "There's a courier service downtown. They open at seven. I'm taking this over there now."

"Okay. Remember what we discussed."

Keith headed into the kitchen to help Karen with the kids.

"I will." He slammed the door and raced to his car. He eyed Melanie's house. She stood at the window. He gave her a quick wave and she waved back.

After they sent the letter all Kyle wanted to do was count down the days until Christmas. He thought and prayed to the Lord asking to hear back from Phoebe. He constantly checked his email and texts. Whenever his phone buzzed his heart jumped for a second, wondering if it were Phoebe. So far, no word. Christmas was a week away. He took a day trip back to Annapolis. He had a second job interview with a firm and they required he come in person. The job interview went extremely well. After the interview he ran a few errands. He'd arranged for the post office to not deliver his mail to his house while he was in Outer Banks. When he stopped at the post office to get the mail that came for his address, he flipped through it. No word from

Phoebe. Keith had mentioned his neighbor was picking up his mail for them and keeping it until they returned. He visited Keith's neighbor to get Keith and Karen's mail. He flipped through the junk mail and Christmas cards, eagerly seeking a word from Phoebe. Nothing.

Maybe she'd sent a couriered letter to their home addresses. Neither he or Keith would've been at their Annapolis address if she'd couriered a letter there. He sighed. If she'd properly read their letter and wanted to contact them snail mail, she would have known to send her correspondence to the Outer Banks. But, Phoebe was an older adult. What if she got confused and tried to send a signature-required message to their homes *before* January first? *Lord, help me not to stress out about this so much.*

Once he'd returned back to his rental house, he felt that everything was a big waiting game. Waiting to hear back about his job interview. Waiting to hear back from Phoebe. Waiting for Christmas to see Melanie.

He went Christmas shopping one day. There was a small toy store downtown. A coffee shop was right next to the store. As he walked by the coffee shop, he spotted Melanie. She was sitting at the back of the shop and she was laughing hard. Looked like she was enjoying coffee with some women. Probably some girlfriends from church if he had to guess. She looked happy and carefree. He turned away, not wanting to be caught staring.

He quickly entered the toy store. He scanned the aisles until he found something he thought Peter and Mark would enjoy. He purchased a toy car for each of them. One blue. One red. The sales clerk charged his credit card. "Would you like these gift wrapped?"

He nodded. "Yes please." He watched her as she wrapped the presents. He'd made a good choice. He was sure Peter and Mark would enjoy these. He chuckled to himself. He could imagine Mark trying to snatch Peter's car, even though he had one of his own.

Holding the shopping bag with the wrapped toys, he went into the jewelry store across the street. He needed to get Melanie a gift. After scanning the jewelry, he spotted some small gold dove shaped earrings. A tiny diamond winked in the middle of them. Perfect. He'd give these to her on their Christmas date. Even if she opted not to spend time with him, he still wanted her to have something nice. She deserved it.

"Would you like this in one of our Christmas gift bags, sir?" He paid the cashier for the earrings. On second thought...

"No gift bag. Thanks." He accepted the earrings which were in a plain white bag and the receipt. As he exited the jewelry store he mentally kicked himself. He couldn't give Melanie these earrings for Christmas. If things worked out between them then maybe he could give them to her for Valentine's day or some other occasion. Sure, she was awesome and he wanted her to have them, but, if he offered them as a gift on Christmas day then he could imagine her thinking that he was trying to bribe her to go out with him.

He didn't want to give her the wrong impression.

He wasn't sure what to give Keith and Karen. He'd have to think about that for a bit. He continued scanning the shops until he spotted Marceline's, a fancy French restaurant. Perfect. He knew exactly what he needed to purchase for them.

When he returned home that day, he placed the boys' gifts underneath the tree.

He removed the cream-colored envelope from Marceline's from his shopping bag and placed it into his drawer. Keith and Karen seemed so busy with their kids. When did they take time to...well, he imagined they'd want to go have some fun, wouldn't they? One day, a few days before Christmas, after they'd fed the kids their lunch they were about to put them down for a nap. He decided now was a good time to give them their gift. He would make them an offer he was sure they wouldn't refuse. "How about the two of you go to the movies?" He'd overheard Karen telling Keith about a new chick flick that had recently come out. She wanted to go see it sometime after the holidays – when they could find a babysitter for the twins.

Keith frowned. "Are you sure?"

He shrugged. "Yeah. I've watched your routine since you've been here. I know what to do."

Karen frowned too. "I'm not sure. I think I'd be worried and not want to watch the movie."

Well, he'd do his best to convince them. "The theater is down the street. If you get an angry text from me, you can be back in five minutes. The next show starts, for that movie you wanted to see, in a half hour. So, if you take advantage of this you'll be able to make it in time if you hurry up and get ready." He offered the cream-colored envelope to Keith. "Think of this as my Christmas present to you. After the movie you can have dinner at Marceline's. I've heard their food is fantastic."

Karen gasped. He quickly looked at her to be sure she was okay. "Keith. We haven't been out to a restaurant since the twins were born." She grinned. "I'm getting excited. Thanks, Kyle." She hugged him.

They rushed and got ready. The kids were already asleep when they left. The twins woke up an hour and a half later. Sometimes they cried when they woke up and sometimes they just moved around and made gurgling noises. He took them out of their playpen. Man, they were heavy. He quickly changed their diapers. Phew. After Kyle had washed his hands he cleaned their fingers with baby wipes. Mark started walking to the kitchen – his steps shaky and uneven.

He looked at Peter who crawled behind his brother. "Peter, I'm sure you'll be walking soon."

"Ga." The boy replied and grinned. He wiped the drool from the kid's chin. Since he'd been spending time with them, he could now tell them apart. Peter tilted his head a certain way. Mark didn't always listen and he wasn't very friendly. Sometimes he'd snatch a toy while Peter was playing with it. Karen or Keith would step in and reprimand him whenever he did that.

They "talked" if you could call it that. He couldn't understand what they said. The only understandable words he'd heard so far were 'hi' and 'mama'. He eyed the contraption that he needed to strap them into to eat at the kitchen table. After naptime they always had a snack. Well, he didn't want to risk strapping them in wrong. What if they fell down and busted their heads on the kitchen table? He'd feel awful about that and surely Karen would be mortified.

He spread a blanket on the living room floor. "We're eating in here today, buddies.

We're having a picnic." He put down a towel over the blanket just in case they made a mess. He again cleaned their hands before they ate their grapes and crackers while sitting on the floor. They drank apple juice from their sippy cups. Karen had cut the grapes in half. To him that seemed time-consuming. She'd patiently explained that grapes were a choking hazard for young children.

Once they were finished with their snack they played with their toys. He sat on the couch and watched them. He turned the TV on to a cartoon channel. Mark abandoned his toy to look at a cartoon. Peter crawled over to Kyle and looked up at him. Kyle started to pick him up but he started crying. "Well, you're sitting there staring at me. Thought you wanted some attention." Peter looked over at Mark who was enthralled with the TV show. Peter pulled himself upright and clung to the couch cushion. He'd seen him do that a lot. He then toddled toward his brother. "Ga."

"Hey, Peter's walking." How exciting. He quickly got his phone out and patiently waited. "Peter try to walk again." Later he crawled over and pulled himself up and toddled the few steps toward his brother. Kyle sent Karen and Keith a text. *Peter's walking!* He made a video of Peter walking and quickly shared it with Keith and Karen.

He then got down on the floor and hugged both of the kids. They wiggled out of his arms. He kissed both of them on their chubby cheeks. Maybe he could be a family man someday. Seeing Peter's first steps made his heart burst with pride. He hugged them again.

20

Christmas Eve

Kyle stirred the melted marshmallows and chocolate for his Rocky Road Dreams candy. While it was still warm he added cashews and pretzels and the rest of the ingredients. Right before it was completely cool, he added extra marshmallows. He lined the gift box with wax paper and placed the freshly-made candy into the decorative box.

Keith came into the kitchen and yawned. "What are you doing making candy in the middle of the night?"

He assumed the scent of chocolate woke his brother up. "Just something I need to do."

"That's a lot of candy."

"Yep."

"Why'd you put it in a gift box?"

"Because I need to." Hopefully Melanie would accept his Christmas gift.

Christmas Day

Melanie opened her eyes. Five AM. Today she was supposed to meet up with Kyle. She yawned and eyed her phone. A text from Kyle? Sent at twelve AM? Curious, she opened the text.

Mel, we're meeting up today. I'll bring coffee and pastries to your house at seven am, if that's okay. I can come later if you wish.

She quickly texted back.

See you at seven.

Once when she was a kid her class had gone on a field trip for science. They'd watched butterflies hatching. Her stomach felt like a million of those critters were fighting for space in her stomach. *Lord, please don't let me get sick.* She needed to calm down. She didn't even know if she could stomach coffee and pastries this morning. Karen had already told her to come by for Christmas dinner later, so, it made sense for her and Kyle to meet up this morning.

After washing up she looked in her closet. What should she wear? She changed her outfit three times before settling on a simple pair of jeans, comfortable walking shoes, and a winter white sweater. She put her hair up into a bun and put her makeup on. Her hands shook. Oh, she needed to calm down.

The loud rap at her door made her jump. She took her time walking to the door. When she opened it her eyes widened. Kyle carried a Christmas gift wrapped in red festive paper. He wore a dark suit and white shirt. He had on a dark blue tie. Looked like he'd recently gotten a haircut and his beard was trimmed. He looked downright handsome. She sniffed. He smelled amazing. Oh, how she'd missed the wonderful smell of his cologne. "Merry Christmas, Mel." He leaned toward her and kissed her cheek.

She finally managed to find her voice. "Merry Christmas. Come in."

She then noticed he had a shopping bag. They went into her kitchen. He placed the gift onto the table and removed the coffees and the box of pastries from the bag. She pressed her hands together. Goodness. She'd not been expecting them to exchange gifts. She'd not gotten him anything. The flutter of butterflies drifted through her stomach again. She said the first thing that popped into her mind. "I'm too nervous to eat."

He smiled at her. "So am I."

She blew air through her lips. "I didn't get you a gift."

"That's okay." They sat on the kitchen chairs. "I'd like for you to open my gift before we talk if you don't mind."

She nodded as he handed her the wrapped box.

Curious, she ripped off the paper and saw the plain white box. She removed the lid and the scent of chocolate and sugar spilled from the box. It was a huge box of Kyle's Rocky Road Dreams candy. It smelled terrific. But why did he give her a box of candy as a gift? Before she could manage to ask him he leaned toward her. "You said you didn't get me a gift. I was going to ask if you'd give me the honor of spending time with you as my Christmas gift." She furrowed her brow. Before she could ask him to further explain he took both of her hands into his. He looked directly into her eyes. Man. His eyes were so nice and hypnotic. "Melanie. I'm falling for you hard. I've thought about you every day since I rented the house across the street. I'm giving you this box of candy because I want to share it with you. Every day through New Year's I want to come by and spend an hour with you. We could share some of this candy." He looked away as if embarrassed. "Or, if you think it's a bad idea for us to be alone we can simply take a walk on the beach. I want to get to know you better." He took a deep breath. "I've found a job in Annapolis and I start in mid-January. You'd mentioned that you'd be relocating back to

Annapolis in the New Year?"

She quickly nodded. "Yes, I'll be—" he put his fingers over her lips.

"I need to get all of this out before I lose my nerve. I know you're worried about my drinking. I understand that. I can't promise that I'll never mess up, but, I'll be sure to try my best. Things are looking up for me. I fell off the wagon when Earl died. But, I haven't touched alcohol since. Except for the alcohol that Chloe spilled on me at Thanksgiving." He took another deep breath. "Just consider granting me the gift of your time and I promise that I'll do everything within my power to make you happy when we're together."

When he stopped speaking, looking at her, she figured he was waiting for her response. She gulped and squeezed his hand. "Yes."

He stood up and whooped so loud, she wondered if Keith and Karen could hear him across the street.

Man, she looked so amazing. As they shared their coffee and pastries, he told her everything about his mom and Phoebe White. She looked surprised as he dished out all of the details of what had occurred since he'd rented the house across the street. "So, you haven't heard from Phoebe?"

He shook his head. "The courier service has confirmed that Phoebe White signed for the envelope." Since she'd agreed to their spending time together, he wanted to be sure he told her everything. "Keith was worried that I'd start drinking if Phoebe rejected us. I told him that I won't do that."

"Have you been going to AA meetings?"

"Not since I've been on the Outer Banks. I'll return to the AA meetings when I go back to my house in Annapolis." She nodded at that. A relief that she didn't look very worried. "How about you?"

"I'm going to be moving back to Annapolis sometime after the first of the year. I have a friend in Annapolis whose roommate recently got married. She told me that I could move in and become her new roommate. The marketing firm where I used to work hired me back." She grabbed his arm. He loved how she would grab him or touch his hand whenever she was excited or wanted to make a point. "Actually, I saw they'd posted my old job as open. Kyle, I've been gone for less than a year. Apparently, they'd filled my position after I resigned but the new person wasn't a good fit for them. The staff had been lamenting about how much they missed me. When I saw the posting I reached out and they were more than eager to take me back – with a raise and a promotion."

"Congrats, Honey." They shared a brief hug. "What about your herb shop? Are you content to put your dreams aside for now?"

"I want to own my own shop, but I'll do it another time, on my own terms." She picked up her phone and accessed a website. She showed him the site on her phone. A nice picture of her, with bottles of herbs, was at the top of the site. "I've started a health food and vitamin blog. I don't have many followers yet but, I'm trying. I also found a trusted company online that's linked to my blog. I get a percentage commission for all the food, herbs and health products that are sold to people from my blog."

"Mel, that's wonderful. Congrats."

"Thanks, Kyle."

He glanced at his phone. They'd been

sitting there for three hours. They were having Christmas dinner at two and Melanie had already told Karen she was coming. He needed to head back to do the last-minute preparations for their meal. He took Melanie's hands and leaned toward her. They kissed. Her lips were the sweetest thing he ever tasted.

21

Kyle sprinted down the coastline of the beach with Melanie. The wind whipped around them as their sneakered feet made footprints in the wet sand while they jogged. He playfully caught Melanie and hugged her hard. She laughed. They briefly kissed before making their way back to her house.

It was almost nine AM on the day after Christmas. Christmas day had been memorable. After they'd shared breakfast, he returned to his house and finished making preparations for the mid-day meal. After eating roasted turkey with stuffing and all the trimmings all of them had sat in the living room all day, talking and having a good time. Mel had sat beside him on the couch. It was good having her there beside him for Christmas. At times, he had to ignore the urge to pinch himself to make sure he wasn't dreaming. Being with Mel was like a dream come true and he'd do everything within his God-given power not to mess this up.

He'd visited her early that morning because she needed to do stuff in the store all day. She'd planned on keeping the store open later that evening, eager to get rid of all of her inventory before the store was officially closed for good. When he'd initially arrived she'd suggested a walk on the beach. He'd eagerly agreed.

After he'd kissed her good-bye he returned to his house. The twins were crying in the living room. He overheard Karen telling Keith that Mark had tried to steal Peter's toy car and the two had started fighting. The boys made enough noise to wake the dead when they cried out at the top of their lungs like that. "Cut it out." Keith's voice echoed in the living room and the kids immediately stopped crying.

Keith was pushing the last two of their mother's boxes over to the couch. He glanced at Kyle. "I figure we can start going through these today."

He nodded towards his brother. "Sounds good."

A hard knock sounded from the door. Hmm. Maybe he'd forgotten something over at Mel's and she came to return it? He opened the door. A male courier stood at the doorway holding a large white envelope. "I'm looking for Kyle or Keith Baxter."

"I'm Kyle Baxter."

"Sign here please." He quickly signed and the courier left.

Kyle's heart kicked into overdrive as soon as he closed the door and scanned the envelope.

It was from Phoebe White.

"Man, what's wrong?" Keith came over to him. Kyle's hand shook as he handed Keith the envelope.

Keith looked concerned. "She responded." He paused for a few seconds before glancing at Kyle. "You okay man?"

Kyle nodded. "Yeah. I want to open it now."

"Okay."

Since the kids were still making some noise they went into the office in the back of the house. Keith closed the door and they plopped into the two office chairs in the room. Keith gestured toward the envelope. "Did you want me to open it or did you want to do it?"

Kyle closed his eyes. "You can do it. Can you read it out loud?"

"Sure." Keith pulled the corded string at the top of the envelope and opened it. Inside was a single sheet of white paper.

"Dear Keith and Kyle Baxter,

I appreciate your reaching out to me. I would like to meet with you. I wish to explain why I gave your mother up for adoption. You had mentioned that you were curious to meet me? I'm curious to meet you, too. Are you able to come to Ginger Falls? I don't travel outside of the area as much as I used to. But I can do so if that is the only way to meet you. I wanted to ask if we could meet at the location below on December 29th at 1:00? I understand if you need to choose an alternate date. Please text or email my grandson Greg if you would like to confirm, or to request an alternate location, date and time. My grandson's contact information is below. I'm afraid I do not use a computer nor do I have a cell phone which is why it is best if you contact Greg.

Phoebe White" He then recited the contact information at the bottom of the letter.

Kyle gulped. "Wow, she wants to meet us. I feel so nervous."

Keith nodded. "Yeah, I'm a little bit nervous too."

Both of them were silent for several minutes.

"Looks like we have a...a cousin or something? Greg would be our cousin, right?"

"Yeah. He would be our cousin."

"Keith, I know it's only a few days away and both of us are on vacation, but I think we should go. We could fly to Philadelphia and rent a car and drive to Ginger Falls for the meeting. We could fly back that evening."

"You're sure?"

"Yes." He needed to explain why he didn't want to wait until another time. "As you know, I start a new job in mid-January. I'd like to do this now while I'm off. I can process and think about everything before my new job starts." He took a deep breath. "Do you understand? I don't want this hanging in my mind, wondering, when I start my new job."

"I understand man." Keith stood up and shoved his hands into his pockets. "Let's do it."

The plane touched down on the tarmac at Philadelphia International Airport. Kyle's stomach suddenly felt upset. He'd not had much to eat that morning he was so nervous. They picked up their rental car from the airport. Keith signed all of the documents and got the keys for the car. "You want to drive, Kyle?"

"No, man, you can drive."

While Keith got behind the wheel and

started the one-hour journey to Ginger Falls Kyle laid his head back on the seat and closed his eyes. He'd felt a bit off since they'd decided to meet with Phoebe. Melanie noticed he'd been moody. The last few times he'd seen her hadn't been as joyous as their beach walk on the day after Christmas. The pall of uncertainty was like a mist over their former ecstatic mood. Mel had been so thoughtful and patient. She said that things would go well since Phoebe seemed eager to meet them – he should not feel scared about meeting her. She told him not to worry and to pray about it. They'd gone to the movies one night. It was a movie he'd been wanting to see. His mind had been so preoccupied that he'd barely paid attention to the film.

He'd been analyzing *why* he wanted Phoebe to like them so much. He sensed that Keith would've been content with not reaching out to Phoebe. But, Kyle knew it would always bother him if he'd not ever made the effort to contact Phoebe. He thought about their childhood. Their wild days. There dad was working a lot and didn't always properly supervise what they were doing. Their dad had raised them alone, along with Ms. Sonia, their housekeeper. Ms. Sonia had told him and Kyle about Jesus and salvation. Neither of them had initially listened. Keith had finally found Christ when he was in his twenties. Keith had shared a deeper bond with Ms. Sonia than Kyle. Ms. Sonia had taught Keith to cook. She was the closest thing to a mother they'd ever had.

But, he'd never considered Ms. Sonia to be his mother. She was married and had a family of her own. She worked for their dad on the weekdays cooking and cleaning. As adults, he and Keith visited Ms. Sonia whenever they could. She was still a part of their lives, and he liked the connection they shared with her. He figured that since Ms. Sonia was not his mother, and he never really had a mom since she died when he was three, well...deep down, he felt that was a missing part of his life. Perhaps it was like a hole that needed to be filled and he mistakenly wanted Phoebe to fill some of that hole. "I can't think of her as my mom."

"What'd you say?" Keith pulled off of the highway, making their way toward the exit, closer to the spot where they'd be meeting Phoebe White.

He didn't realize he'd spoken his thoughts

aloud. He shook his head. "Nothing."

Both of them wore dark blue suits and ties with their good polished black leather shoes. Both Karen and Melanie had taken pictures of them before they left. For some reason, Melanie opted not to go to her herb shop that day. She'd mentioned when they were leaving that she was spending the day with Karen and the boys. "I forgot to text Melanie that we'd landed."

"That's okay. I texted Karen. I'm sure she'll let her know. I think Mel understands that you're nervous."

They finally parked in front of the place where they were meeting. It was a restaurant and Phoebe's grandson had texted them the previous day, letting them know that Phoebe had reserved a private room for their lunch appointment. They were over an hour early. They waited in the car until it was time to go into the restaurant. The hostess took them to their reserved room in the back of the restaurant.

Phoebe had not yet arrived.

The wait staff brought them ice water and served them bread and butter. Kyle tapped his foot. He glanced at the rolls. He just couldn't eat right now. Maybe after Phoebe arrived and they started talking, then maybe he'd be able to eat something.

He kept tapping his foot and rubbing his hands together.

"Hey, calm down Kyle."

"Where is she? She's fifteen minutes late."

"So? Maybe her grandson got stuck in traffic or something."

Keith sent a text to Phoebe's grandson. No response. He then called him. The call went straight to voicemail.

Anxiety jumped through him like the release of a tightly coiled spring. *Man, if I ever needed a drink it's now.* He pushed the unwelcome thought away. Once they'd been waiting for forty-five minutes, he shot out of his chair.

"Kyle. We made a long trip. We need to wait a bit longer."

"Okay. I'm just going to go outside and take a quick walk." He needed to calm down. The wait staff had already asked if they wanted anything to drink. He could really use a gin and tonic about now. He rushed outside, not bothering to put his winter coat on. The cold wind blasted against his hot skin. He shoved his hands in his pockets and paced in front of the restaurant. *Lord, help me. Lord help me.* He chanted the words. Checked his phone. It'd been an hour. It was two o'clock and it looked like Phoebe decided not to show up. He sighed. Maybe she was sick or maybe she'd changed her mind.

She was elderly, so maybe she was in the hospital or something? But, why didn't her grandson pick up his phone and let them know?

A black car pulled up in front of him. The man, looked to be the same age as he, got out of the backseat of the car and rushed to the passenger side of the car and opened the door.

The man helped Phoebe to get out of the vehicle.

22

She wore a black dress and pearls. She carried a dark purse and she had a small hat on her head. She waved her elegantly-gloved hand in front of her face. "Oh, I'm so distressed. How could this have happened. Greg, you should have been more careful."

"Grandma, I couldn't help it if my car broke down and my phone wasn't charged up."

"Oh, I hope they didn't leave." She looked directly at him and stopped. Her mouth dropped open. She placed her gloved hand over her now-quivering lips. "You're...you were in front of my house earlier this month. You were in a parked car." She frowned. "Or, was that your brother?"

Might as well tell her the truth. "It was me. I was surprised that you were White."

"Oh, my." She chuckled for a few seconds, and then she laughed. Her blue eyes twinkled when she looked at him. Without asking permission, she hugged him. He hugged her back. She smelled like some kind of flower, a strong scented flower. She gestured toward the young man. "This is my grandson Greg." Kyle politely shook Greg's hand.

"I'm Kyle Baxter." It was such a relief that she showed up.

Greg threw his hands up in the air. "My car broke down. My phone wasn't charged up. We were outside of town on a side street. I had to walk to get help. I called a friend of mine and he arranged for an Uber to pick us up." Kyle just now realized that the car that had dropped them off had driven away.

"Grandma, don't forget your coat." He now noticed that Greg was holding her coat. Kyle took the coat from Greg's outstretched hand. Kyle opened the door and the threesome entered the restaurant. He led them to the back room where Keith patiently waited. Keith stood up as soon as they entered.

"Oh my." She eyed both of them up and down. "Both of you are so handsome." She then grinned. "I'm a hugger. Can I give the you a hug, Keith? I already hugged Kyle outside."

She hugged Keith before Greg introduced himself. "Hi, Keith. I'm Greg." Greg hugged both of them briefly. He then explained to Keith why his grandmother was over an hour late for lunch. "I'm going to let Grandma visit the two of you alone. I'll be at the coffee shop next door if you need anything."

Phoebe made herself comfortable and they discovered that she'd already ordered an elegant meal for the three of them the previous day. "If you don't like what I ordered just let me know and we can get you something else." She looked at both of them.

"I'm not aware of your religious beliefs. Would one of you bless the food, if you feel comfortable doing that?"

Sounded like she was a Christian. Perhaps that'd make this whole visit so much easier. "I'll do it." Keith volunteered. "Lord, bless the food we are about to receive. Kyle and I appreciate the opportunity to meet Phoebe White, our biological grandmother. Please be with her throughout the day. Please let your Holy Spirit guide and comfort and protect us during this wonderful meal. Amen."

"Amen." Both Phoebe and Kyle responded simultaneously.

While they ate, she asked them lots of questions about themselves. "When you contacted me, I became aware that the child I gave up for adoption was probably deceased." A sheen of tears showed in her eyes briefly before she blinked the moisture away. "Did the two of you have a mom growing up?"

Kyle took the lead and told her about their mother dying of cancer and that their dad never remarried. Keith told about Ms Sonia. "She was the closest to a mom we had."

"It was a blessing that Ms. Sonia helped to care for you. Is she still alive?" They both confirmed she was still a part of their lives. She asked a multitude of other questions. What were their likes and dislikes? Keith told her he was a pastor and told her about Karen and showed her pictures of the twins. She smiled when she saw their pictures. Kyle told of his profession and mentioned Melanie, stating that she was a woman he'd just started dating. She continued asking a multitude of other questions. Kyle wanted to remind her to tell them about their mom and about why Phoebe had given her up for adoption.

Before he could ask, Ms. Phoebe gestured toward one of the wait staff. "Could you bring me a bottle of port?" She glanced at the twins. "Sometimes I like to drink a bit of port for dessert. You two should have some. It's good."

Port. Dessert wine. How he loved a good glass of port. He could use a glass right now. But if he enjoyed one sip, he'd be drinking until the sun came up. Bad idea. He was afraid if she got a bottle and put it on the table, he'd be staring at it craving a glass and not be able to focus on their discussion. He cleared his throat. "Uh. Ms. Phoebe." He wasn't sure what they were supposed to call her. Didn't feel right to call her Grandma, at least not yet. "Would you mind not ordering the port?" He took a deep breath. "I'm an alcoholic and, well, I'm nervous right now and need a drink but should not have one."

"Oh, my word. I'm so sorry." She quickly told the wait staff not to bring the port. "I don't mean to make you feel uncomfortable. Kyle I'm so glad you told me. I'll be sure to keep that in mind for future visits."

Oh. Sounded like she wanted to see them again. That sounded good. "I know I've been asking the two of you a lot of questions. I figure that you have a lot of questions about your mother, rest her soul." She took a deep breath. "My marriage was not always happy. I don't feel like telling you all that was wrong between me and my husband. I had an affair with the janitor that worked at the school where I taught. I thought he was amazing. I wanted to leave my husband and run away with my boyfriend." She stopped eating and took a deep breath. "The janitor, your grandfather, ended up abruptly leaving the school and moving away. But it wasn't his fault." She took another deep breath. "My husband was on the school board. He accidentally found out about my affair and had my boyfriend fired." She shook her head. "It was so awful. We fought and argued and then I discovered I was pregnant. My husband knew the child wasn't his and he didn't want to raise a Black child plus he was bitter."

Kyle leaned toward her. "He was bitter because you were unfaithful?"

"He was bitter because we'd been trying to have a child for years and had been unsuccessful. I thought I was a barren woman and that I'd never have kids, but, lo and behold, I had your mom." She shook her head. "Even though my husband had multiple faults, I did love him. I agreed to put the child up for adoption and agreed to work on our marriage." She sighed. "At the time, I wasn't sure if I'd be strong enough to give the baby up for adoption." She pressed her gloved hands together. "Two years after I gave birth to your mom my husband and I had one child. Connor. He's an architect and he lives in Texas. Greg is Connor's son."

Keith took a drink from his water glass. "Does Connor have other children?"

She nodded. "He's got a daughter named Molly. She lives in Alaska. Both of my grandchildren are still single and they don't have any kids."

Kyle leaned toward her. "What was our grandfather's name?"

"His name was George Brown." She took a deep breath. "When we dated, he mentioned that he lived in foster care for most of his life and didn't have connection to any of his family." She took another deep breath. "I'm afraid that I don't have any pictures nor did I keep in contact with him. I honestly don't know where he's living or if he's even still alive."

Kyle tucked the information into the back of his mind. He was still digesting meeting Phoebe and making sense of his life. He honestly didn't know if he wanted to try to find his grandfather. Perhaps he and Keith could discuss it sometime way in the future.

Keith checked the time on his phone. "Kyle and I made a long drive here from Philly. We need to get back and catch our flight home this evening."

"Oh my goodness. I've been yacking away not paying attention to the time. Could you do me a favor and text my grandson and tell him to come back to the restaurant? He said he'd get me one of those Uber cars to take me home."

Keith texted as requested. All of them stood up. She hugged both of them. She looked directly into both of their faces. "I want to see you. Regularly if you want. I have a good feeling about you and I'd like to meet your wife and children Keith. Kyle, I'd be honored to meet Melanie."

She gave them her phone number and encouraged them to call whenever they wanted and hinted about having all of them to come to her house for a get together one day.

After one last hug, Kyle and Keith left the restaurant and got into their car. As they drove to the airport Kyle thought about their visit. "You okay, man?"

"Keith, if you ask me that one more time..."

His brother shrugged. "Sorry. You know I'm worried about you."

"Don't worry. I'm fine." They drove in silence for several seconds. "She seems nice. Talkative. She seems caring. Do you think she really meant it about having all of us to her house for a party?"

Keith shrugged. "Not sure. People will say they'll do something and then not come through. Even if she doesn't come through and do it, I believe she intended to do it. Know what I mean?"

"Yeah." He closed his eyes. He'd not slept well the previous night, worrying about meeting Phoebe. Glad they'd made the decision to meet up with Phoebe, he yawned and fell asleep.

Six months later...

Melanie entered the posh-looking restaurant. The walls were a deep burgundy color and tiny lights twinkled from the ceiling. Each table had a single candle in the middle and a nice view of the water greeted her as soon as she walked in. Wow, this place was so amazing. The hostess approached. "May I help you?"

"Yes. I'm meeting Kyle Baxter."

The woman grinned. "Right this way."

Melanie followed the hostess, still drinking in the amazing décor of the restaurant. Kyle stood up as soon as he saw her. Wow, he looked so handsome. He wore his dark suit, crisp white shirt and navy-blue tie. She noticed a few women in the restaurant giving him admiring looks. She wanted to scream at those ladies: *He's mine.* He clutched a bunch of vivid red roses. "Hey Melanie. Happy birthday." He put the roses aside and leaned over and hugged her hard. Oh, how she loved being held in his strong arms. He released her and kissed her cheek.

"Hi, Kyle." He pressed the flowers into her arms. She sniffed the wonderful roses. He held her hand as they sat. "This restaurant is so nice. It's such a treat to eat here for my birthday."

He grinned and gave her a quick wink. "I wanted to make sure you had a good time on your birthday."

He looked flustered. He'd not picked her up for her birthday dinner because he said he'd been working on a special project and didn't want to be late for their date. She'd agreed to meet him at the restaurant. "Did something happen? You look like something's bothering you."

He quickly shook his head. "No, I'm fine." Their server approached with their food. She assumed he'd placed their orders before she'd arrived. "Mel, you look amazing."

She grinned. "Thanks Kyle." Whenever Kyle gave her a compliment, her heart pounded with joy. It made her feel good, warm and toasty whenever he said positive things about her. His compliments were sincere – coming straight from his heart. That's just one of the reasons why she loved him so much. He was kind, caring and truthful and she was addicted to seeing him regularly. Whenever he went on a business trip or had to leave town she always missed him like crazy. She'd worn her favorite white summer dress with flats. She loved the way the white material clashed against her brown skin. She wore the dove earrings he'd gotten her for Valentine's day. They were her favorite piece of jewelry and a lot of her girlfriends had complimented her on them. "You look nice, too."

"Thanks. How's everything been going? Your blog still doing good?"

Wow. He always asked about things that were important to her. She loved that about him. "Yes. I received two hundred more followers over the past week. Kyle, I can't believe how much my blog has taken off since Christmas." She'd also been able to sell a lot of herb and vitamin supplements through her blog. No, she wasn't making a living doing it yet, but she had a good start. She loved that she wasn't beholden to Uncle Larry any longer. She was doing this herself and that gave her a feeling of independence.

He nodded as he sipped from his water glass. "That's good. How's Chloe been doing? Did you take her for her sonogram visit?"

She nodded. "She's doing fine." Chloe had to take it easy during her pregnancy. Either herself or Uncle Larry accompanied Chloe to her doctor visits. Chloe still confided to Melanie when she needed to. Melanie was glad that she could be a friend to her young cousin. "She still hasn't decided on a name for her baby." They'd already found out that she was having a girl. They'd discovered via social media that Drake had already had two other girlfriends since he and Chloe had parted ways. Both Uncle Larry and Melanie had convinced Chloe for her health's sake, and the baby's sake, that she should not reach out to Drake – not until he got help for his anger issues and his drug problem.

He nodded. "Glad to hear that."

"Are you excited about the cookout at Phoebe's house?"

He grinned. "Yes. I can't wait to meet the rest of her family."

Kyle and Keith had been corresponding with Phoebe since they'd initially met a few days after Christmas. Melanie, Karen, and Keith's twins had met Phoebe earlier that year. She thought Phoebe was a kind and caring woman and she was glad that she wanted to be a part of Kyle's and Keith's lives. She could tell that Phoebe's acceptance was important to Kyle. She was having a huge summertime cookout later this month and she was eager to attend as well.

They continued talking until they'd finished their meal. Kyle held her hand. He still seemed a bit nervous, so she figured maybe something was going on at work. She was about to ask him about it when he dropped to the floor on one knee. She gulped, speechless. "Melanie. I love you. I've loved you for a long time. Dating you is not enough for me anymore. I want to marry you. Will you do me the honor of accepting my marriage proposal?"

He pressed a small box into her hand. She

accepted it into her shaky hands. Wow, she'd not been expecting this. Joy, as pure and plentiful as spring rain, exploded within her. "Oh, Kyle, I love you too. I love you so much. Yes." She said the single word so loud that other diners looked toward their table and clapped. Her hands were shaking she was so nervous. Kyle helped her to open the ring box. The brilliant solitaire diamond sparkled. He slipped the ring onto her finger. He cupped her face with his large hand, leaned toward her and kissed her until she was swooning with exquisite happiness.

23

Twelve months later...

Melanie felt as if she were gliding on air as she slowly walked down the aisle of the church. Her wedding dress was exquisite and when she spotted Kyle, her heart leaped into overdrive. As she continued walking toward her groom, she couldn't help reminiscing about the past twelve months.

She glanced at Chloe, who had agreed to be one of her bridesmaids. Her young cousin looked elegant, beautiful and happy. A single mom, Chloe stayed with Uncle Larry with her nine-month-old baby girl, Aisha. She'd managed to find a job at a local daycare facility, so, she took Aisha with her each day for work. She'd confided to Melanie that she was thinking about becoming a kindergarten teacher. Chloe had really matured, especially since Aisha had been born. Drake was currently serving time for assaulting his girlfriend. His career never took off in spite of his efforts.

As she slowly continued down the aisle she thought of Phoebe White. They continued spending time with her. She was a sweet woman and she'd become a close family friend. As they bonded, she could imagine Keith's twins calling Phoebe great-grandma one day. Phoebe had graciously accepted their wedding invitation and her son Connor, and his kids, Molly and Greg, also attended the wedding. They were like an extended family and she was glad that they were a part of their lives.

She looked directly at Kyle. He looked so handsome in his tux. Just before they said their vows, he flipped her wedding veil over her face. He leaned toward her and whispered in her ear. "I love you."

"I love you," she whispered back.

If you enjoyed Rocky Road Dreams, then I'd appreciate it if you left a sweet one or two-sentence review on Amazon, Goodreads, or Bookbub! Reviews are often used by readers to find wonderful books.

Spread the word by sharing my website (ceceliadowdy.com) with your friends and on social media! Thank you!

Read the entire **Candy Beach Series**! https://ceceliadowdy.com/the-candy-beach-series-landing-page/

About Cecelia Dowdy

CECELIA DOWDY is an Amazon bestselling author who lives near Washington DC. She enjoys listening to old tunes with her husband and chauffeuring her teenaged son to his school sports events. Baking is one of her favorite passions. She loves expeimenting with bread recipes using her sourdough starter. Serving homemade desserts to friends brings her joy. Her love of baking shines in her romance novels. When she's not in the kitchen, or spending time with her family, she's cooking up delicious faith-filled plots. Fans say reading her tasty novels makes them hungry. Sign up for her newsletter.: https://ceceliadowdy.com/sign-up-for-my-email-list/

www.ceceliadowdy.com

Connect with Cecelia Dowdy

Join my mailing list! I will keep you updated about future releases:
https://ceceliadowdy.com/sign-up-for-my-email-list/

Let's discuss the Bible – visit my Sunday Brunch biblical discussions on my blog:
http://ceceliadowdy.com/blog/category/sunday-brunch

Please visit my website for more of my books:
www.ceceliadowdy.com/

You can also find me on social media:
https://www.facebook.com/CeceliaDowdyAuthor/
https://twitter.com/cdnovelist
https://www.bookbub.com/authors/cecelia-dowdy
You may write to me at:
Cecelia Dowdy
Divine Desserts Publishing LLC
PO Box 951
Greenbelt, MD 20768-0951

Other Titles by Cecelia Dowdy

THE BAKERY ROMANCE SERIES

http://ceceliadowdy.com/bakery-romance-series/

Loving Luke *(Book 0)*

Raspberry Kisses *(Book 1)*

Shades of Chocolate *(Book 2)*

Sweet Dreams *(Book 3)*

Sugar and Spice *(Book 4)*

Southern Comfort *(Book 5)*

Sweet Delights *(Book 6)*

Cinnamon Kisses *(Book 7)*

THE CANDY BEACH SERIES

https://ceceliadowdy.com/the-candy-beach-series2/

Caramel Kisses – *(Book 0)*

Chocolate Dreams – *(Book 1)*

Milk Chocolate Kisses – *(Book 2)*

Bittersweet Dreams – *(Book 3)*

Coffee and Kisses – *(Book 4)*

Rocky Road Dreams – *(Book 5)*

STANDALONE TITLES

http://ceceliadowdy.com/books/

The Baker's Bride – a historical romance novella
The Doctor's Bride – a historical romance novella